I0699799

Holly & Heartbeats

Working for Love, Book 6

Amber W. Lynne

Carnelian & Quills

This book is a work of fiction. Names, characters, places, and incidents are the product of the author's imagination or are used fictitiously. Any resemblance to actual events, locales, or persons, living or dead, is coincidental.

No part of this publication may be reproduced, stored in a retrieval system, or transmitted in any form by any means, electronic, mechanical, photocopying, recording, or otherwise, including but not limited to text and data mining or the training of artificial intelligence systems, without the prior written permission of the publisher or author, except as permitted by U.S. copyright law.

To request permissions, contact: AmberWLynne@gmail.com

Edited by: Krissy Espindola (KrissyEspindola@gmail.com)
Cover Art by: Rebecca Ruger (BeckandDot@gmail.com)
Paper: ISBN 978-1-960479-32-7
eBook: ISBN 978-1-960479-27-3
Text Copyright © 2025 by Carnelian & Quills Publishing
All rights reserved.

To all the hopeless romantics that can't resist a ridiculously sweet holiday romance and are still working on finding their happily ever after...

...may joy and love find you in entirely unexpected ways!

Chapter One

Jessica

A tub of mint chip sat like a quiet accomplice on the counter, sweating under the kitchen lights. Jess knew—without pretense or illusion—that eating straight from the container in her softest pajamas didn't count as celebrating. Especially not at Christmas time.

Her clinic was closed for the holidays. She had no idea what to do with herself, but she couldn't ask her staff to keep working just because she didn't know how to take a break. The spoon bumped against the carton as she scooped aimlessly; her laptop was nearby with half a dozen open tabs about charity gift drives, rerun holiday rom-coms, and a too-earnest article titled, Ten Ways to Love Being Alone Over the Holidays.

None of it appealed.

The living room was quiet; with only the soft glow of the twinkling lights she had set on a timer. She hadn't bothered putting up a tree, just the lights and a cinnamon-scented candle burning out of habit. Her cozy bungalow in Serenity didn't feel as warm when every room echoed more than usual, and she had nowhere else to go but to the next room.

Her phone buzzed once on the table.

She didn't need to look. She already knew.

Jackson.

A text. Then a call.

Jess let it ring twice, then picked it up with practiced ease. "Hey."

Still pretending that building your own gingerbread clinic out of graham crackers and 'Sarcasm counts as self-care?' Jackson's warm, familiar voice came through with a lopsided grin. She didn't need to see to hear.

Jess leaned back against the counter and let her eyes close for half a second. "If that were true, I'd be certified by the American Board of Baked Architecture by now. No gingerbread tonight, though. Just...freezer aisle therapy."

There was a pause filled with background noise, Molly probably laughing softly in the distance.

Jess softened. "How's she feeling? Still holding that baby hostage?"

"Yep," Jackson exhaled. "Due any day now. She's trying to decide if the baby needs antlers on its hospital cap."

Jess laughed, then bit down on it, warmth swelling and tugging something low in her chest. "Sounds like her."

There was another thoughtful pause before Jackson added, "You sure you're okay spending the holiday alone?"

She could hear the frown in his voice. That old protectiveness she used to lean into without thinking. He knew the only family she had was a found one, and that, without her friends, she'd be alone.

"I'm good, Jackson. Seriously."

"I just…" he trailed off, then shifted. "You've been there for me every Christmas since—well, since a decade ago. I know we aren't 'us' anymore, but we've kinda had a tradition."

She glanced at the condensation pooling beneath her untouched ice cream.

A breath hitched in her chest—unbidden—and suddenly she was back in her old kitchen, three Christmases ago.

Jackson had burned the crescent rolls *again*. The timer was ignored as she danced around the tile, Bing Crosby crooning from his speaker. She'd been half-dressed for a shift at the clinic, laughing as he spun her under the garland strung above the cabinets. Her pager buzzed—two sharp jolts against her hip—and everything froze.

"Don't," he'd said, catching her hand before she could reach for it. "You promised. Just this morning."

She hesitated—just a second. But her career always came first, didn't it? Patients didn't care that she'd stayed up until the wee hours hanging ornaments or that the stuffing was still cold in the middle. There was a flu outbreak. A pregnant teenager in her third trimester. No coverage.

Jess had kissed him on the cheek, grabbed her keys, and whispered, "I'll only be gone an hour."

He smiled, soft and tired. "You said that last time."

She hadn't made it back until well after dark.

The holiday rolls ended up in the trash, along with the tinsel he'd tried to hang on the mantle. That night, he curled up with the leftover ham she barely touched and watched Miracle on

34th Street alone before falling asleep on the couch.

She remembered standing in the hallway, coat still on, watching his shoulders from behind and thinking, *this isn't what either of us asked for.*

And that was their problem. She hadn't offered him the same commitment Molly had…Jess hadn't given him a family.

Now, the candle on her counter flickered, and the cheap wick sputtered.

Jess pulled the ice cream closer and took a slow, steady bite, the mint sharp on her tongue. They no longer celebrate that version of Christmas.

Not anymore.

"We did." Jess let the truth settle on her tongue, steady but kind. She'd grown and taken a few lessons from him, too. "But this year is different. You and Molly are starting something new."

"That doesn't mean we can't still—"

"It means I want you to have this fully," she said gently. "The waiting. The chaos. The antler caps. All of it."

Jackson went quiet. When he spoke again, it was softer. "And what are you going to do, Doc?"

There it was.

Jess swallowed the hollow ache forming behind her ribs. "A date with a blanket, a movie about improbable holiday miracles, and possibly the worst whipped topping known to mankind." Her smile never quite reached her voice. "Don't worry about me."

We'll do better next year. We'll find other traditions…when things aren't so new.' She could hear him sigh softly through his nose.

"We always do." Molly scooped out some softened ice cream from the carton. "I've got to get back to my creamed ice before it melts."

"Alright," said Jackson, resigned.

"Tell Molly I said she's got this."

"She's got this," Jackson agreed. "And Jess, seriously. If you change your mind—"

"I won't."

He didn't push further. That was the difference now—he knew when to let her go.

When the call ended, she set her phone down next to the carton and gazed at the laptop. The blinking cursor waited on the half-read article. She closed the tab without reading another word.

Carrying the carton and laptop, Jess moved into the living room and settled onto the couch, her legs curled underneath her. The remote was across the room, deliberately out of reach—a self-imposed test of willpower from earlier that now just felt more like an inconvenience.

No voices. No music. No clatter of baking. Even the candle's flickering flame felt underwhelming.

The silence wasn't solitude anymore.

It was hollowness. It was the absence of anything that mattered or brought a semblance of holiday cheer.

She'd done holidays alone before. Even last year, she'd shown up at Jackson and Molly's with a ham and hung a few ornaments on their tree. But this? This year, they didn't need her. Which was good. Progress. Everyone deserved that joy.

What she hadn't realized—what now lived in her doubt—was how much of her holiday spirit had always been borrowed from others' moments. She'd never actually created her own. She rubbed her wrist absently with her thumb—the calming trick she used between patient triage and 2 a.m. newborn check-ins.

Pulling the laptop to her knees, she clicked open a new tab without thinking and typed: *Christmas retreats near me.*

Enter.

A cascade of links loaded with spa weekends, yoga getaways, and silence lodges.

But just above the scrolling list was one small photo. A cedar-shingled house strung with white lights. A wreath on a fence. *The Holly House Inn.*

The site was simple. It featured a few photos of an old wooden porch and a fire-lit parlor, but no big-city branding. Just soft light, pine boughs, and a kitchen that looked like a dozen generations of grandmothers had baked holiday treats there.

The tagline made something soft unravel for her.

Wrapped in tradition, with the promise of home.

It was simple. Honest. Jess had built her life on reliability—on steady plans, clean breakrooms, and framing patient charts like puzzles she was trained to fix. She had spent years helping others while quietly setting aside her own wants.

Truth was, she didn't know what her own traditions looked like.

The ones she'd grown up with had faded after college, and the ones with Jackson...those belonged to someone else now.

Someone who wore fuzzy socks on Christmas morning and belly-laughed through burned biscuits in a home bursting with future.

This. The site promised something gently impossible for someone like her: a holiday without pretending. A space that was already warm. A quiet place to miss no one and nothing, because it wouldn't expect her to carry the entire holiday season alone. She could enjoy the holiday without a plan preset by someone else.

It had been a long time since a holiday week had sounded like a gift instead of a task.

She re-read the tagline once more, slower this time.

Wrapped in tradition, with the warmth of home.

And for reasons she couldn't name, her throat tightened.

Jess didn't give herself time to hesitate.

Click. Reserve.

She barely acknowledged the confirmation before gently closing her laptop and gazing into the steady flicker of her candle.

She wasn't running away from the solitude of her little home. Not exactly. She'd find new traditions at The Holly House Inn, and maybe, for a change, make a few of her own.

Chapter Two

Jessica

The next morning, Jess was only half-watching a holiday rom-com, legs curled under an afghan with a heating pad pressed against her lower back. The movie featured a fashion journalist who found love beneath a string of fairy lights with a flannel-wrapped woodworker. It was unapologetically festive. And yet, Jess found herself more absorbed in the laptop balanced precariously beside her than the movie itself.

She clicked the trackpad and stared again at the confirmation email.

The Holly House Inn. Five nights. December 21 through 26.

It sounded like a made-for-TV movie: cedar shingles and snow-dusted porches, jingle bells on the doorknobs, and a parlor centerpiece of a twelve-foot spruce tree sparkling as if it had an exclusive deal with the North Pole. There were cocoa bars, handcrafted ornaments, and a holiday happy hour featuring homemade eggnog.

It seemed...obnoxiously charming.

And yet. When she clicked the "Book Now" button, she didn't allow herself to think about all of that. Now it was real. A vacation. Alone. At Christmas. Should she cancel? Or, should she take a solo holiday escape from the ghost of Christmas Comforts Past?

Jess looked toward the bathroom and sighed. Cedar Glen might be in Texas, but it has enough elevation to get real snow. Her usual wardrobe wasn't meant for altitude or wind chill.

She chewed on her thumbnail, eyes darting to the window. Outside, Serenity continued as if nothing had changed. It looked the same every year: garlands strung between lampposts, snowless pines twinkling over storefronts, and a wreath on the bakery door. There was no doubt Candy would be elbow-deep in batter. Bailey and Rosie were probably folding napkins in the shape of trees. And Taylor?

Taylor would know what to wear.

"Are you planning a mountaintop awakening, or just running away to be discovered by a handsome Christmas tree farmer?" Taylor asked, arms crossed as Jess grabbed a sweater the size of a small quilt from the rack.

"Neither," said Jess, though she was blushing slightly. "Probably."

Taylor gave her the once-over and plucked the chunky knit from her hands. "This says you're preparing for emotional hibernation. Let's try something with shape."

She replaced the blanket-sweater with a forest-green funnel-neck tunic with subtle copper threads woven into the hem.

"Festive without announcing it," Taylor approved.

"I'm not trying to be festive."

Taylor raised both brows. "You bought flannel pajamas with reindeer on them and a peppermint bubble bath shaped like a candy cane."

"I was stress-shopping."

"You're adorable when you pretend you don't care."

By the time everything was packed into a sleek roller bag—complete with wool socks, fleece-lined leggings, and one very questionable beanie—here are 'Boots,' she said, shimmying a box closer. 'Lined, waterproof, and distressingly expensive."

"I can't justify this."

"Consider it a gift," Taylor said with a wink. "From your future, happier self."

Jess blinked and tightened her grip on the smooth leather of the boot. The faux-fur lining looked like it belonged in someone else's life, someone who spent holidays with family and sipped hot cocoa, rather than working back-to-back shifts and facing an empty clinic fridge. She'd always prided herself on being self-sufficient. She was too grounded to need surprises or traditions. But lately, the quiet hasn't been peaceful. It was sharp-edged. Lonely.

What was she even doing? Spending money on furry boots for a holiday trip that started as an impulse and now felt like—what? A grieving process? A rejection of everything she'd built—just because she didn't want to spend Christmas watching someone else's happily-ever-after unfolding on her TV?

Still, she touched the leather again and imagined herself in some snow-covered nook, curled up by a fire—not because she needed to escape, but because—maybe for once—she just wanted to listen to her heart.

She exhaled slowly. Maybe she wasn't settling this time. Perhaps she was taking what she wanted.

"Thank you," she said, voice steadier now.

Taylor smiled. "It's about time you let yourself enjoy something just for you."

"I enjoy stuff."

With a knowing smile, she said, "Okay, you're now fully equipped to survive a serene, snowy inn, and all its holiday excess. Except..." Taylor stopped packing bags to look at her friend. "Are you sure you want to be alone for Christmas?"

Jess ignored her and, instead of answering, carefully rolled up a pair of red flannel pajamas and slid them into her overnight bag with the tag still on. "I think I need to be," she whispered.

"Okay." Taylor gave a slight nod. "Just...promise me something."

Jess stilled.

"If it starts to feel good, let it," Taylor said. "You don't always have to fight peace."

By the time Jess left the boutique—her rolling suitcase packed and a garment bag over her shoulder—dusk had fallen over Serenity. On a whim, she took a detour from Main Street and stopped at Patty Cakes.

Inside, Candy was frosting something blue, white, and shaped like a snowflake. She looked up just as Jess approached the counter, brushing a smear of white icing from her cheek.

"Well, well, Dr. Louis," Candy teased. "Tell me you're not skipping town just because our version of a white Christmas is a little heavy on the fog."

"Guilty," said Jess with a smile. "I've decided I need a dose of nostalgia and maybe a cookie as big as my face."

"Say less." Candy disappeared for a moment and returned with a snowflake sugar cookie that filled the dessert plate. She nodded toward Jess's suitcase and armful of clothes. "So, what's the plan? Spa getaway? Extended house call for a mysterious case of the holiday blues?"

Jess hesitated. "Just...a change. I'm heading to this inn in the hill country called Holly House."

Candy blinked, then slowly grinned. "Oh, you're serious. You're doing the 'Christmas in the country' thing."

"I'm observing it," Jess said airily. "Passively. While sipping cocoa and maybe journaling under a heated blanket."

Candy exchanged a glance with Taylor, who had just joined them, apparently following Jess.

"You're going to come back with a fiancé and a cat," Candy said solemnly.

Jess rolled her eyes, but she was laughing. "No animals. No impulsive decisions. Just some peace and quiet."

Right. You forgot something," Taylor said, dropping a square box into Jess's tote. "And just in case serenity turns into romance...wear the red flannel. It plays well on wooden staircases covered in garland.

Jess didn't unpack the joke—or the box. She'd let Christmas surprise her.

That evening, under the gentle glow of her bedside lamp, Jess finished packing. Along with her jeans and cozy sweaters, she added her new stylish winter boots. A spritz of her favorite perfume. A small hardcover book of poems she hadn't read in years.

The flannel pajamas went in last.

She looked at her suitcase, studying it with a mix of worry and hope, then zipped it closed.

Chapter Three

Jessica

Tendrils of wind curled beneath Jess's cardigan as she stepped into the breezeway in Amarillo and out into the rental car lot. She pulled on the thick winter coat Taylor had helped her choose. The faux-shearling trim brushed her cheek while she waited in line. She signed the rental paperwork with stiff fingers, already feeling the cold in a way she hadn't experienced back in Serenity. The lot outside stretched wide and flat, with rows of cars blinking under a pale afternoon sun. She found her SUV—modest, all-wheel drive, already running—and whispered her thanks to whoever had turned on the pre-heated seats.

Once she merged onto I-40 eastbound, the steady hum of tires on asphalt, soft holiday music from her playlist, and the quiet click of her fingernail against the steering wheel filled the cabin. The roads were dry today, but the digital highway sign just outside of town warned: WATCH FOR ICE. She adjusted her speed, watched the sky for signs of change, and kept her grip steady.

Highway 287 stretched northward in a long arc, and the landscape shifted. The buildings became sparser, replaced by open pastures outlined with wire fences and occasional red barns that dipped slightly in the wind. The playlist she had pulled up on Spotify filled the car with cheerful holiday tunes—an ideal soundtrack to match the rustic scenery.

By the time she saw the old wooden sign welcoming her to Cedar Glen, the sun was low enough to cast a golden glow over the hills. Jess leaned forward slightly, watching the land stretch out wide before rising in gentle ridges. Not a mountain—but enough elevation to remind her why she'd packed a wool coat.

She rolled down the window further. The air smelled faintly of greenery and smoke. Lights twinkled along shop roofs, and evergreen boughs wrapped around signposts. A few parked trucks lined Main Street, and behind the windows of a modest bakery, rows of gingerbread men stood like troops. One figure wore a tiny candy cane stethoscope. Jess smiled and thought of Candy.

Despite her nerves, something deep inside eased up.

The world shifted again when she pulled into a roadside gas station—her coffee had caught up to her, and she wanted to stretch her legs. If the pumps weren't vintage, they were high-quality replicas. A handwritten sign out front read, 'Pay at the Counter.' Inside, a wave of warmth hit her face, flushing her cheeks. Tin signs and faded posters lined the walls, and the air carried a strangely perfect mix of motor oil, cinnamon gum, and fresh popcorn.

Waiting in line behind a broad-shouldered man buying windshield fluid and a pack of glittery holiday stickers, Jess couldn't help herself.

"Stocking stuffers?" She asked, nodding toward the stickers with a tilt of her chin.

The man turned with a grin—maybe twenty years her senior, his eyes were merry to match his thick, graying beard. "Twin granddaughters. If it sticks or sparkles, my wife says they need it."

Jess chuckled. "Seems fair."

"Oh, absolutely," he agreed. "Some households run on r ules...ours run on reindeer stickers and bribery. You from the area?"

Just passing by. I reserved a room at the Holly House Inn for a few days.

He perked up, visibly interested, now. "You're heading to the ridge?" At her nod, he added, "Well, you timed it right. They say the snow might actually stick this year. Ridge catches the cold before anyone else. Especially that place."

"Sounds like a solid endorsement."

"You'll like it," he said, ripping his receipt from the machine. His voice shifted, and he seemed to be somewhere else in his mind. "That place was made with love and family in mind...you'll feel it. Just keep your eyes open for holiday magic."

Jess raised a brow. "Holiday magic?"

"The ridge," the man said with a playful shrug. "The ridge has a way of catching people off guard. Especially, with Graham and the girls in charge."

"Graham," she repeated slowly.

Tall fella. Beard. As expressive as a fence post. Good guy, though. Keeps the place running. And he's got those girls of his to help—you'll recognize them when you see them." He gave a knowing smile and a small wave. "Enjoy your stay."

The door jingled as he vanished into the cold.

Back on the road, Jess turned up the music and followed the highway back out of town. Jess wondered what kind of man came with a local weather warning.

About five minutes later, her GPS's friendly female voice directed her to turn left onto a narrow road that led straight to Holly Ridge. As the pavement gave way to a thin layer of gravel, the trees drew closer, their pine boughs arching overhead. The GPS went silent—and that's when she felt it: the breath she hadn't realized she'd been holding slowly started to release.

When she rounded the final corner, the inn came into view. Cedar-shingled and two-storied, it stood with quiet charm, its wide wraparound porch strung with white lights that glowed warmly against the dark green shutters. A wreath hung in each window, decorated with red holly berries and neatly tied ribbon bows. The gravel lot had been carefully leveled, with minor wooden signs marking spots for guests and staff.

She sat for a second, breath deepening, hands curled on the wheel.

"No expectations," she whispered, even as her stomach dipped. "You're here to rest."

Boots crunching on gravel, she headed toward the wraparound porch. That first step onto the wide, weathered planks creaked a welcoming sound.

She knocked lightly, then tried the door. The latch clicked. The door eased open, not all the way—just until she heard a voice squeal, "Someone's here!"

Jess blinked.

At the bottom of the wide staircase that cut through the foyer stood two girls, identical in size and shape but different in every other way. One held a stack of paper snowflakes, her braids smooth and perfect. The other had wild hair with glitter on her cheeks and wore a tutu over green and white striped leggings.

Jess gave a small wave. "Hey there."

Before either could respond, a calm voice echoed from beyond the hall. "Girls, leave the guests to check in, please."

A moment later, a man appeared. Tall. Wearing flannel. His beard just shy of neat. He held a clipboard in one hand and had a serious look that wasn't quite hostile, but definitely not warm and friendly.

Jess knew before he said another word. His reputation preceded him.

Graham.

"Dr. Jessica Louis?" he asked.

"Jess is fine," she replied, brushing windswept curls out of her eyes. "I have a reservation."

He nodded silently, only gesturing toward the front desk, a polished counter beneath framed black-and-white photos of snowy landscapes and children with wrapped gifts.

"Welcome to the Holly House. You are in the Juniper Room."

He handed her a brass room key tied with a sprig of green ribbon. No printed tags or plastic. Just old-school charm.

"Thank you. It's beautiful here," she said, glancing toward the shining tree in the corner.

"Appreciate it," he muttered quietly.

As she leaned toward the guest register, the twin with the perfect braids moved closer and stage-whispered, "She doesn't look very fun."

Her sister elbowed her. "You're not supposed to say that out loud!"

Jess fought a smile and offered a wink. She could be fun.

Graham sighed—not unkindly—and motioned vaguely toward the staircase.

Go up the stairs on the right. Breakfast is served from 7 to 9 in the sunroom. The activity schedule is posted in the parlor—there, around to the left.

"Thank you."

"Anything you need, you can ask me, Clara, or Noelle. Enjoy your stay," he said, then, without any indication of which twin was which, he turned and walked off, disappearing down the hallway under the stairs with purposeful steps. "Girls, with me."

As they exited the room, the wilder of the two turned back and silently mouthed "I'm Noelle" with a face as expressive as if she had screamed it.

Alone, Jess stayed for a moment longer, her eyes drifting toward the tall entryway tree. The lights blinked slowly—steady and warm—creating a cozy scene.

The inn felt like a storybook.

But the innkeeper?

He was hard to read.

Returning to her room, she felt like stepping into a snow globe. A white coverlet, red piping, and a wreath on the window trimmed with fabric snowflakes. A welcome card, written in tidy script, rested on the nightstand. She ran a finger along the words.

Please, make yourself at home.

She ran her fingers over the words, wondering if it had been left by Graham or the tidier of the little girls; the other didn't seem to be the type to focus on careful penmanship.

As she unpacked, the muffled sound of laughter drifted through the floorboards. Jess paused and reflected. "They all seem to be having fun. Maybe I should join them?"

When she left her room, she sensed the house shift. Not literally—though the air had cooled behind the cedar-shingled walls—but metaphorically. Something in her softened as she closed the door to her room, held the heavy brass key in her hand, and took in the peaceful atmosphere of Holly House Inn's second-floor hallway. A garland traced the railing downstairs with pinched red velvet ribbons. Each brass room number gleamed subtly under soft sconce lighting.

She moved carefully up the stairs, pausing briefly on the landing to watch the firelight flicker in the foyer below. From the far end of the hall—clatter of cutlery, muffled laughter, the clinking of teacups. Something about the sounds drew her forward, past the foyer, and toward a sign reading 'Parlor + Morning Hospitality.'

The 'hospitality' part made Jess smile, even as her ribs squeezed tight. Graham had seemed more hostile than welcoming, but the kids and the house...that felt right.

Inside, the parlor's windows were dark, but warm light from mounted sconces and candles illuminated the room with a yellow glow. Mismatched mugs filled a tiered rack above a long sideboard cluttered with coffee carafes, tea tins, and small crocks of honey in a basket. Nearby, a tray of chocolate chip cookies and a small sign labeled "Help Yourself, Help Others" sat on a folded stack of red gingham napkins.

A quiet murmur filled the space, not crowded but lively. At one table, a young couple whispered to each other between sips of cocoa—wedding bands catching the light as they gestured mid-sentence. Nearby, a girl no older than six carefully sorted candy canes by size at a side table while her dad scrolled through his phone with a sheepish look.

To Jess, it felt like walking into the middle of a story that wasn't hers.

Still, her fingers curled around one of the mugs, and the scent of clove-studded orange gently rose from an open tea tin.

"You're here for the holiday package, aren't you?"

Jess turned to see a woman in her sixties wearing cranberry cords and a wildly festive sweater covered in singing carolers. A 'My Name is' sticker on her lapel read: MRS. D.

Jess smiled. "For better or for worse."

"Is this your first time here?" Mrs. D asked warmly, taking a mug of tea for herself.

"Yes." Jess nodded. "The website for Holly House was irresistible."

"Oh, you're going to love it here! My husband and I have been coming ever since we were as young and foolish as those two." The old woman waved at the newlyweds canoodling in the corner. "Are you here alone?"

"Um—" The panicked look on Jess's face must have been enough to give her an answer.

"I'm sorry!" she said, as a blush filled her cheeks. "That was rude of me."

"Mrs. D—"

"Please, you can call me Helen."

Helen, I'm Jess. She shook her head. "It's okay. Yes, I wanted to have a traditional holiday."

This place is special. You're going to have a lovely time," Mrs. D. patted her arm. "You must've met Graham. Don't let his frosty edges fool you. He thaws around Christmas brunch.

Jess laughed. "He's a whole mood."

Helen leaned in, her voice soft. "Are you playing Bingo?"

"Bingo?"

Honey, at Holly House, you'll play games and craft like they are Olympic events and be sneezing glitter by the 24th. That's the whole point. Welcome ritual. Distraction. Joy on a plate. You'll see.

Jess blinked, unsure whether she was more alarmed by the promise of sparkling boogers or relieved that it was apparently expected to feel overwhelmed at first.

"Does your husband participate?" Jess asked.

Mrs. D laughed. "Lord, no. We come every year. The same week, the same suitcase, the same husband who always forgets his slippers. That's him over there asleep in the wingback chair." She pointed toward a peaceful man dozing with a crossword perched loosely in his lap. "He likes that we both get to relax and enjoy the holidays, and he doesn't have to do anything to entertain me! I like meeting new guests. I guess I'm the unpaid welcome committee."

I'm going to look at the activity sheet tomorrow. I don't know what I'll do, but I guess I...needed this.

Helen lightly tapped her cup to Jess's in a quiet toast. "We all do, sweetheart. We all do."

Later, when she stepped out onto the porch for a breath of fresh night air, the cold kissed her cheeks with a gentler chill than she'd expected. The sky had turned into a velvet navy, dotted with stars peeking through wispy bands of cloud. Below, Holly Ridge sloped gently toward the softly lit town, just visible through dark trees. Jess crossed her arms loosely over her chest and leaned against one of the porch's wide, wrapped columns, letting the coolness clear her mind.

The night air carried hints of pine and burnt firewood. Peaceful. Quiet in a way that didn't feel empty...just settled.

Footsteps scuffed just off the side path, then a deep voice echoed through the air. "Girls! Gloves, now!"

She peered around the porch and saw Graham emerging from the shadows near the side stoop. A long scarf was looped twice around his neck; shoulders hunched from the cold but standing firm. There was something in the way he moved that reflected the house: no-nonsense, quiet, built to last.

Then, the burst of movement—a blur of childhood energy spilling through the side door as the twins bound out. Clara, always ready, was already gloved, her braid bouncing as she trotted after her father. Noelle, true to form, wore her gloves tied to her coat cuffs like wings, her earmuffs slightly askew, bouncing with every wild, uneven step.

They were joy in motion. Jess found herself smiling without meaning to.

Clara tipped her head up at Graham as they reached him, and he adjusted her collar with a small tug she probably didn't notice, then reached down to straighten one of Noelle's mittens. He didn't say much. He wasn't warm, exactly, but he wasn't cold either. Or distant. He was just...watchful.

And Jess, wrapped in the darkness of the porch column, realized she hadn't come all the way up the ridge looking for someone to create perfect holiday joy. She wasn't here for declarations or dazzling hospitality. What surprised her—the thing she hadn't counted on—was how much she enjoyed observing without needing to fix anything.

She didn't know what she expected from the innkeeper when she'd booked this trip. Maybe someone less grumpy than Graham Walker. At the bare minimum, someone who barely noticed she was there—but instead, he saw everything. He just didn't respond to it.

He made space like a man who never asked for thanks, just hoped he'd done enough.

Graham looked up then, sensing her presence—maybe—or just pausing as he always did just outside of things. Their eyes met briefly. A flicker in the dim porch light—a beat not long enough to last, yet not quick enough to forget.

She offered a nod. Not a smile. Not a wave. Just a quiet acknowledgment that said: I see you, too.

He returned it with a subtle nod of his chin, then turned back toward the path, guiding the girls toward the outbuildings with a quiet patience you wouldn't notice if you weren't paying attention.

But Jess was paying attention now.

She lingered on the porch for a moment longer, breathing in the fresh country air as the light from the house behind her cast a warm glow over the boards beneath her boots. She didn't feel lonely—not anymore.

Later, in her room, Jess curled up on the coverlet, a blanket tucked around her shoulders. Her mind wandered. Graham and the girls seemed to have all the pieces needed for a Norman Rockwell home...except one.

Where was the girls' mother? Divorce, adoption, death?

No matter the story, one thing was clear: Graham had truly mastered the role of a single father. Even alone, he had created a loving home for the girls. A home that already felt like a warm welcome to her.

As sleep pulled her under, one last thought surfaced: Maybe she could discover the perfect holiday tradition at Holly House.

Chapter Four

Graham

"Be careful!" Graham hollered, as he led the girls into the woods behind the inn. The bare branches above them cast thin, pale shadows as the afternoon faded into evening. The crunch of frost-covered leaves and pine needles under their boots scattered any nearby wildlife as Clara and Noelle sprinted ahead, twin bursts of energy fueled by winter's cold and childlike exuberance.

"Last one to the creek is a rotten egg!" Noelle shouted, twirling a crooked stick she'd claimed as her magic wand. She swung it dramatically, narrowly missing a low-hanging branch as she squealed with delight.

Clara adjusted her scarf with a furrowed brow. "You promised Grandma you wouldn't get us lost. Also, rotten things are disgusting."

Noelle's eyes sparkled beneath her oversized earmuffs. "Then you don't want to be one! I'm way faster than you!"

Graham shook his head, amusement flickering behind his

tired eyes. "Noelle, you might be quick, but remember what happened when you tried to outrun the turkey last Thanksgiving. Spoiler alert: you can't."

Noelle gasped, then flailed her arms. "That turkey was an outlaw! It was a gobble gangster! He was fleeing his execution."

"Eww." Clara sighed as she knelt to scoop up a handful of dry pinecones, inspecting each one like precious treasure.

"You don't think you have enough pinecones already?" Graham said with a half-smile.

"No, Dad," Clara shot back, eyes serious. "You must have *just* the right one. You don't know which one that is, so you have to have lots."

"Is a hundred enough to pick from?" he asked, arching an eyebrow. "I'm pretty sure you're close to that."

Noelle lowered her voice to a whisper, leaning close. "If we don't use them for crafts, we can use them for weapons later."

Clara shuddered dramatically. "Maybe against the bears."

"Bears?" Graham chuckled. "Well then, we'd better make sure we get plenty."

Noelle glanced up at him. "Do you think the new girl guest will make crafts with us? She seems nice."

Clara nodded, turning toward the porch where Jess was collecting pinecones. "She looks like she enjoys messes."

"She laughed when I spilled glitter everywhere," Noelle added with a grin. "That's a good sign."

The girls hurried over to a low patch of moss, and the three of them started gathering treasures. Clara was careful picking out symmetrical pinecones that would be perfect for a fancy mantlepiece. Noelle, on the other hand, tossed handfuls of sticks and stones into her basket freely, stopping now and then to balance a tricky pile with a grin.

"You know," Graham said, hoisting a crooked branch with exaggerated care, "when I was your age, I collected shiny rocks. Mostly just to irritate my sister."

Clara frowned. "Did your sister have magic sticks like Noelle?"

"Does a bear poop in the woods?" Graham countered, winking.

"Gross!" Noelle said. "We're walking in a bear bathroom!"

"Yeah, watch where you step," Graham agreed solemnly. "Stepping in poop is an official badge of wilderness coolness."

Clara rolled her eyes but smiled. "Whatever helps you sleep at night, Dad."

Graham laughed, the sound low and warm. "Sleep is overrated. But you two aren't."

Noelle tossed a bright red berry into the basket and looked up at him. "Do you think Grandpa and Grandma will like what we bring them? Like, really like?"

"I know they will," Graham replied, kneeling beside her. "You're putting all your magic into these."

"I'm going to add a little sparkle," Noelle announced, brandishing an invisible wand over her find.

Clara shot her a sharp look. "Two types of sparkle, remember?"

"No more," Noelle promised, sticking out her tongue.

Graham watched them, his chest swelling against the cold. These ragged, shimmering moments were the true heart of the Holly House for him. Not the perfectly hung wreaths or the stacks of wrapped gifts, but the laughter echoing beneath the evergreens, the worn mittens held tight in tiny hands, and the wild imaginings of two pint-sized queens ruling over an enchanted forest.

His gaze drifted upward to the darkening sky where the first stars began to peek through the tree branches.

His life was filled with everything he had—the inn, the tiny hands in his own, the shared jokes about bear poop and sparkly rocks—but a warmth was steadily growing beneath his ribs. Something aching to be shared.

He gently squeezed Noelle's hand. "It's getting dark. Let's head back before the bears come out to use the bathroom."

Noelle shrieked and dashed away, her stick held high like a spear. Clara pursued her, laughter ringing out loud.

Graham stayed a moment longer, sensing a premonition in the night air. There was something coming.

Chapter Five

Jessica

The smell of woodsmoke and fresh coffee woke Jess up.

For a full minute, she wasn't sure where she was. The Juniper Room's leaded glass windows softened the morning light, casting gentle shadows across the white shiplap walls and brass four-poster bed. No pager. No clinic buzz. No need to rush.

She blinked again. Holly House. Cedar Glen. Right.

Below, the floorboards creaked. Light footsteps—small, quick ones—and a muffled burst of laughter drifted up through the floorboards. It gently pulled her back into her body.

She smiled faintly, stretched long, and eased out of bed.

Jess padded over to the braided rag rug near the bed and reached for her slippers. No need to rush—after all, this was vacation. But her curiosity was louder than her resistance to moving. She'd slept better than she expected and, surprisingly, was eager to go downstairs and see who else was awake.

Downstairs, the inn was already in motion.

The sunroom, now serving as a dining area, was filled with

morning light pouring in from the frost-lined windows. All the morning noise seemed to come from there. The same man and young girl from last night's nightcap in the parlor were now sitting with his wife and toddler—who squealed happily as he dipped his toast into cocoa. Across the room, the newlyweds from yesterday were snuggled together in a window seat, whispering and giggling over their shared pancake stack. At a central table, the unmistakable voices of Clara and Noelle floated above the morning buzz.

Jess crossed over to the buffet table where a small tray of fresh scones waited, alongside stacks of fresh buttermilk pancakes and a pitcher of maple syrup warmed by a tea light. Two carafes of dark roast were labeled Bold and Bolder. She poured a cup of Bolder.

She scooped a scone onto her plate, not entirely hungry but happy to hold onto something warm. Throughout the room, faces glowed with early-morning cheer. She lingered uncertain—until a hand waved her over.

"Saved you a seat!" Helen crowed.

Jess smiled, sliding into the chair. "Good morning, thank you."

"Of course," Helen said, topping off her coffee. "I was fairly certain you'd join us. You've got an early-bird vibe. Practical shoes. Alert posture."

Jess laughed. "I overslept, actually. It's almost eight. That never happens."

"Well, that, my dear, is the sign of a good mattress," Helen replied. "The three best things about Holly House: hot scones, good company, and no expectations—except to have fun."

Jess tore a piece from the edge of her scone and took a bite. "Feels like the perfect combination for a restful holiday."

Helen offered a knowing nod. "Exactly so."

From the center table, syrup drama unfolded.

"Noelle," Clara groaned, "use the tiny cup. How many times do I have to remind you, syrup is not a beverage?"

"I'm not drinking it!"

"You're drinking it."

"I'm not—! I have a lot of pancakes!"

"Better than cable," Mrs. D murmured affectionately, watching the twin drama unfold.

Graham appeared near the buffet, running a hand through his beard while murmuring to a man wearing a work shirt and tool belt. His flannel shirt was layered beneath a dark vest, and his brow furrowed as their conversation grew more intense. But when Noelle squealed about her syrup tower collapsing, he instinctively half-turned, his eyes drawn toward her.

That look—the automatic calibration of a father mid-breakfast, sensing chaos—softened something in Jess that she hadn't realized needed warming.

She looked away before her curious gaze could be considered staring.

"You'll get used to him eventually," Helen said, catching her expression.

Jess raised an eyebrow. "Is that so?"

"The gruff? The withdrawn thing? Part of the charm. He's not rude, but he hasn't had much practice. Especially when it comes to new guests."

Jess put her fork down. "Let me guess—he thrives on

schedules, laminated lists, and practical problems that can be solved with power tools?"

Helen chuckled. "Bingo, and you're lucky. This is chill mode. There are fewer guests than usual. Usually, we're full up. Mr. Walker—Graham—says the questionable weather reports discourage some folks from making the drive."

"Bad weather?" asked Jess. In her impulsiveness, she hadn't even thought about doing something as responsible as checking the weather. Instead, she just assumed it would be cold and moved on.

The local services are saying there's a snowstorm brewing. Likely, the biggest we've seen in years.

Jess felt a moment of panic. "Should we be worried?" Her doubts about the trip returned in a wave.

"Oh, no, dear," said Helen, patting her hand. "The ridge gets snow, sure—but Holly House doesn't close. Not in 80 years. As long as the generator works and the cocoa flows, we ride it out together. He'll just be a little twitchy until all the candles are counted and he's gone down his checklist. I think he's worried because there's more to do than usual, and a house full of guests expecting Christmas traditions."

Yeah, I imagine it's hard to set up a sugar cookie decorating station while battening down the hatches. Jess let that settle. Ride it out together.

Ten minutes later, Jess finished her breakfast and followed the guests' murmurs toward the parlor. The young couple now lingered by the fireplace, coffee mugs in hand. The chalkboard beside the piano had been updated with large-printed letters:

HOLIDAY TRIVIA: 12 p.m.

DIY SNOWGLOBES: 2 p.m. (with cocoa!)
GINGERBREAD HOUSE DECORATING: 4 p.m.

Jess studied the board...This wasn't a passive, slippers-and-silence kind of retreat. It was scheduled joy. Structured whimsy.

"Are you signing up?" A small voice echoed up from her hip.

Noelle blinked up at her, glitter still clinging to one cheek. Clara stood just behind her, hands behind her back as if apologizing already.

Jess gave her the side-eye. "Are you trying to pressure me into holiday crafting?"

Noelle nodded thoughtfully. "Grandma Jackie said crafts are how your soul exhales."

"That is...a very insightful and mildly intimidating thought."

"You should really do the snow globes," Clara said, coming into view now. "Mine last year had pinecones and a toy moose named Marvin. He floated funny."

"Floated?"

"They leak a little if you don't get it all the way shut. Daddy forgot to tighten my lid."

"Mine too," Noelle piped up cheerfully.

Jess chuckled. "Poor Marvin."

"He drowned," Clara said reverently.

"I see there are also Gingerbread Houses. Is it too much to do both?"

The girls, in opposition to their usual display of order and chaos, genuinely looked identical—especially in their horrified expressions. Ask silly questions, get silly responses. Noelle spoke first. "You have to do both!"

Clara, taking a moment to gather herself, added more calmly, "Well, no one *has* to do anything, but I mean, why wouldn't you?"

"You're right. I'll do it," Jess said with mock solemnity. "For my soul, and for poor Marvin."

A clipboard appeared from behind the reception counter. A soft thud echoed as Graham stood up and placed it next to a small tray of pens.

"Sign-up sheet," he said to no one in particular.

Jess reached for a pen without thinking, scribbling her name beneath three others: the two girls and 'Sara,' signed in a shaky signature. When she looked up, Graham was gone again, footsteps heading down the back hallway.

That man had the social awareness of a startled raccoon.

And yet, she couldn't stop her eyes from watching him walk away.

Back in the Juniper Room, Jess looked at her packed bag sitting neatly by the closet door. She had brought a novel, two magazines, and a folder of client files she fully planned to ignore. She wasn't quite ready to admit it yet, but the trivia and glitter appealed to her more.

The craft room at Holly House was tucked behind the parlor—a cozy, slightly cluttered space that smelled faintly of cinnamon dough and old projects. Jess stepped inside just as a few guests settled around folding tables covered with snowman tablecloths. Each place setting featured an upside-down mason jar, a bin of plastic figurines, tiny pine trees, and a bottle of what could only be called dangerously optimistic glitter.

The girls had staked out a corner with the confidence of veterans. Clara organized the supplies with quiet precision, while Noelle had already taken off her cardigan and was gluing tiny snowmen onto each of her fingertips.

Jess slid into the empty chair beside them and reached for a mason jar. "Remind me how Marvin met his untimely end?"

"Plastic moose body, heavy glitter, loose lid," Clara said solemnly.

"He wasn't made for the water," Noelle added, as if narrating a Netflix documentary.

Jess handed each girl a tiny pine tree and a tube of superglue. "Well, today's mission is a simple one: no casualties."

Clara adjusted one of the snowmen until its scarf was aligned properly. "I wrote a checklist this year."

"You made a snow globe assembly checklist?"

Clara nodded, pulling a paper from her pocket. "Our dad says failing to plan is planning to fail."

"I say your dad needs a second mug of cocoa," Jess muttered, amused.

The next twenty minutes blurred in a flurry of giggles, elbows, and minor glue mishaps. Jess helped Clara straighten a crooked reindeer and forced a too-tight lid back into place. Noelle, true to her usual self, managed to get two types of glitter in her hair and one googly eye barely attached to her sweater.

Jess had never been so completely covered in craft fallout.

Her sleeves were speckled with iridescent shimmer, her fingers stuck together in at least two spots, and a rogue pinecone tried to hitch a ride in her boot cuff.

But the laughter?

The easy, rolling kind that came from full-bodied joy?

That she hadn't realized she needed. Aside from her time with Jackson, she couldn't remember another occasion when she'd laughed so hard.

"Okay," Jess said, holding up her own jar. Inside, a tiny deer stood near a gold gift box wrapped with a bright red ribbon, and two bottle-brush trees. She had carefully arranged everything so the glitter would swirl in a halo without covering her delicate scene—a proper snow globe for a medical professional, if there ever was one.

Noelle peered into it, wide-eyed. "That one looks like it would make wishes come true."

Jess flipped it and shook it up. "Holiday wishes?"

"You're way better at this than Dad," Clara observed. "He gets stressed about the glue and the mess."

"He also says glitter is contagious," Noelle added, voice quieter. "That it multiplies just like some things called gremlins do if they have water after midnight."

Jess smirked. "He's not wrong."

From the doorway, a throat was cleared. Jess turned—and there was Graham, arms crossed lightly, leaning against the frame. His gaze swept over the girls before briefly settling on Jess.

"Y'all doing okay in here?" he asked, his tone even.

Jess couldn't quite read the flicker in his eyes—or the faint smile that tugged at his mouth when he saw the glitter in her curls and the streak of glue across her arm.

"We didn't make anything explode," Clara called.

"Yet," Noelle added.

Graham let out a sigh like a mother does, but with gentleness Jess hadn't expected. "Don't bother the guests," he said, mostly to the room but clearly watching Jess for her reaction.

"They're not bothering me," Jess said easily, tipping her snow globe toward him. "We're three for three on watertight construction and zero fatalities. Unless you count Marvin, may he rest in peace."

That surprised a crack of a smile from him. Small, but there.

Jess caught the way his eyes lingered on the girls' bent heads, proud and aching all at once.

"Alright," he said finally, voice softer now. "Carry on." He turned, hesitated, then added, "Make sure you maintain glitter containment protocols." Then he was gone, boots moving heavily but unhurried down the hall.

Clara looked up. "He likes you."

Jess added a dot of glue to her snow globe lid, pressed it tight, and whispered, "I think I like him, too."

Chapter Six

Jessica

A jar of rainbow-colored candies rattled as she set it down on the nearest table, narrowly avoiding Noelle's elbow. The smell of gingerbread hung thick in the air—molasses-sweet with a sharp bite of clove.

The craft room had transformed over the past hour. What had started as a tidy, well-stocked workspace is now a glitter-covered battlefield of frosting tubes, crumbled walls, and sugar casualties. No one would be eating these houses unless they wanted a sparkly trip to the bathroom later.

Jess stared at the blank gingerbread foundation in front of her and crinkled her nose. She hadn't meant to build anything complicated. Honestly, her plan was more about pretending to ignore icing licks and munching on a gumdrop or two, under the guise of quality control. But somehow, she had been drafted into full-scale construction.

Noelle declared herself the artistic director, Clara offered a supply inventory system, and after being handed a piping bag and a plan sketched in marker on the back of some construction paper, they clearly proved they were professionals. Jess had rolled up her sleeves and surrendered.

Half an hour later, their gingerbread house wobbled somewhere between whimsical cottage and a calorie-laden shipwreck. Gumdrop pathways zigzagged carelessly. The chimney leaned heavily to one side, as if it had weathered three Texas thunderstorms, and one gingerbread man was perched on a rooftop candy cane zipline. Another had, according to Noelle, met an unfortunate demise in the marshmallow pond. Maybe only one of them was a professional.

"It's magnificent," Jess said, gently rotating the cookie base. She couldn't stop grinning at it.

"It's an inn," Clara explained, hands sticky with remnants of royal icing. "That side has the guest wing—see, with the blue windows? And the tower on top is for making magic cocoa."

"Of course," Jess said, nodding seriously.

"And the marshmallow pond is where people make wishes," Noelle added. "Wishes don't work without sparkle."

"Good thing you used half the glitter tray, then," Jess said, brushing a flake off her sleeve.

"Grandma says we're only allowed two glitters," Noelle confided. "She says more than that is excessive."

"She likes clean crafts," Clara said. "And she likes helping Dad."

"She's old," Noelle added without malice, popping a gumdrop into her mouth.

Clara adjusted a peppermint swirl with surgical precision. "She helps out a lot since..."

Her voice trailed. Too quiet.

Jess set down her frosting tube. "Since what?"

Noelle blinked upward. "Since our mom died."

The sweetness in the air was still for a moment. Clara focused intently on her roof.

Jess paused, unsure if she should speak right away. Clara kept her eyes on the gingerbread, but both girls had fallen silent, a gentle softness settling between them.

"We were babies," Noelle murmured, trying to sound casual but missing just enough that Jess's chest ached. "She's still around, though."

"In spirit," Clara echoed.

Jess swallowed. "I'm so sorry."

"It's okay," Noelle said. "Dad says she loved gingerbread. He uses her recipe."

That's why it smells like real Christmas," Clara added, not glancing up.

Jess reached for a marshmallow and pressed it into place. "She would be really proud of both of you. And of this masterpiece." Her voice softened.

Noelle looked up at her. "You're more fun than most grownups. Even the nice ones don't usually get this messy."

Clara smiled faintly, wiping at a smear of icing on Jess's sleeve. "You're not trying to keep us busy while you do other stuff. You actually like being here."

"I do," Jess said. The admission surprised her. "I really do."

She leaned a little closer, examining the gingerbread house through their eyes. Haphazard, candy-laden. Just perfect.

"Am I doing this wrong?" she asked softly. "Spending time

with you like this? I don't want to...overstep."

Both girls looked up at her and blinked.

"You're not doing it wrong," Clara said.

"I'm not?"

"Nope," Noelle said. "You're just not boring."

Jess laughed quietly. "That's a relief."

Jess smiled, but it was shaky at the edges. She didn't know what she expected from this trip, but it wasn't this—sticky hands, hollow truths, and two tiny voices saying she was doing okay. It unraveled something inside her.

Noelle peeked at it and frowned. "You put a chimney made of marshmallows, but they're all crooked."

"It was the wind," Jess said. "A strong holiday breeze blew through."

"Like at the North Pole?"

"Exactly."

Clara stifled a giggle, and Jess caught it—the spark behind the amusement, the brief way her eyes searched Jess's face like she hoped the moment might last longer than just today.

Jess's throat caught for half a second. She set down her frosting pipe and wiped her hands on a napkin, listening to the quiet chaos around her: the mom and dad trying to help their two young kids figure out gumdrop placement, the pulsing Christmas music from a portable speaker in the corner, the soft-muttered calculations of Clara designing a second-level for her gumdrop stairs.

"I like building with you," Noelle said softly.

Jess's fingers paused on her paper napkin, mid-fold. She turned.

"I do too, Elle."

Noelle grinned. "No one calls me that."

"Oh—sorry, I didn't mean—"

"I like it."

Jess smiled just as Noelle leaned against her in the most casual, unconscious gesture anyone could make—a sugar-coated eight-year-old shoulder pressed gently into Jess's side. She looked up to see Clara's eyes flick to her sister, then back to Jess, as if trying to measure something she hadn't meant to reveal.

Jess had never been the kind of adult that kids flocked to. She didn't do voices. She didn't wear goofy sweaters. She could stitch a wound in four minutes and tell the difference between croup and the common cold by ear alone, but she always believed that genuine warmth was harder to express.

Maybe she had underestimated herself. She had just never allowed herself to have fun.

"You girls holding up in here?" The familiar voice drew her attention to the doorway.

Graham stood with one hand on the door frame. There was a dusting of snow in his beard and a hint of the outdoors on his coat. His jaw looked tighter than usual, as if he hadn't taken a full breath since sunrise, but his voice lacked the tension she'd expected. It was soft.

His eyes swept over the scene—glitter on the table, piped icing mid-spiral, the girls with cheeks pink from excitement—and then landed on Jess. Her sleeves were covered in edible confetti. She peeked up at him, feeling guilty and a little unsure if she was about to get scolded like a kid caught drawing on the walls.

"We were just, um—" she started.

But Graham shook his head, eyes flicking from her fingers to the house. He cleared his throat. "It looks...messy."

Jess opened her mouth again—

He added, "And good. Real good."

Clara brightened. "We put wishes inside."

Noelle clapped her hands. "And glitter in the cocoa tower!"

Graham raised an eyebrow. "Can't have cocoa without glitter, right?"

Noelle nodded furiously.

"You used the entire bag of mini marshmallows," he noted, tilting his head at the sugar-stuffed eaves.

"They were structurally necessary," Clara said.

Jess sipped and licked frosting off her knuckle. "You doubted the vision. That's on you."

A low but genuine laugh escaped him before he stopped himself. "I don't know how y'all did it," he drawled, looking at the organized chaos, "but this reminds me of the time we hosted six second graders and a gerbil for someone's birthday."

"There was only one frosting casualty," Noelle piped up. "And it wasn't me this time."

Clara lifted a hand like she was about to argue that point, then seemed to think better of it.

"They've been excellent," Jess said, brushing glitter off her forearm. "Graham, I think you've raised a couple of architectural geniuses."

Graham's expression softened, pride unfurling through his features like a seam bursting after being pulled too tight.

When his gaze landed on Jess again, she was still watching

him.

Their eyes met.

Something unspoken lingered between them. Not a spark—something softer. More genuine. Like an unwrapped secret, neither of them was ready to face yet.

He gave a nearly imperceptible smile, then said, softer, "Thanks for helping."

"I didn't mean to intrude," Jess replied.

"You didn't," he said. "I've got a few things to double-check before nightfall, what with the storm coming in stronger than expected. This...helps." Appearing uncomfortable, Graham said, "Dinners at six." Then, he turned around and left.

Jess nodded before really considering it. "Of course." She took a breath—and then gave a genuine smile. The kind that sank in somewhere deep and warm. Maybe, just maybe, she wasn't intruding at all.

When Jess turned back to the table, both girls were watching her. Noelle reached over and added a gumdrop to Jess's roof like it was a crown.

Clara leaned her chin on her hand. "You should come back next year."

Jess swallowed.

Then she smiled and began wiping down the table.

"Maybe I will."

Chapter Seven

Graham

Graham looked out the small basement window, jaw tight as gray afternoon clouds thickened and rolled over the ridge.

He hated storms on the ridge. It wasn't the noise, downed trees, or the snowdrifts that piled up and kept them trapped up there. It wasn't even the risk of losing power—modern resources and a big stack of firewood took care of most of that.

No, he hated storms because they meant one thing: loss of control.

He inhaled, drawing in the sharp, familiar scent of cedar, rain, and machine oil, then picked up the chainsaw from the workbench and tested the pull cord. It sputtered, coughed, and then roared to life. Graham let it idle for a moment before flipping the kill switch and setting it aside with a grunt. Check. Wood filled the woodpile. Flashlights and candles were easily within reach. The grocery delivery had arrived that morning, double the usual order.

He scratched his forehead under his beanie and reached for

the clipboard propped against a pile of salt bags. The checklist was almost complete. He flipped the top page, revealing hand-sketched diagrams of the outbuilding paths he'd need to shovel.

He blew out a breath.

The inn had never closed because of bad weather. Not when Margaret's great-grandmother ran it. Not even during Snowmageddon in '98, when the power went out for four days and guests built makeshift snow forts out back. And it wouldn't be now. The inn was a sanctuary, and he would make sure it was ready to shelter anyone who needed the protection of its walls during the storm.

From above, the muffled chorus of voices filtered down—the twins' laughter was the loudest among them. Clara's quick cadence. Noelle's singsong delight. And woven through it all was a third voice he recognized far quicker than he had expected: Jess.

Damn if that woman didn't sneak into a room.

He'd never thought about having someone else help run activities during the holiday season. Margaret had handled everything. And after she passed, he kept it going. Her parents helped at the inn, but they'd always been involved. It made sense that they'd also help with the girls. The twins needed the softness Eleanor brought and the steadiness Walter offered.

But this time? With the storm approaching, asking for help from them didn't feel right.

They'd offered, of course--as stubborn as ever. But he'd said no. It was too risky. Eleanor's hands now trembled when she carried anything heavier than a tea tray. Walter's knees protested the porch steps. They still said yes, every time the girls asked to visit or bake cookies—but the truth was, they were starting to slow down and needed rest more than they needed to come to the rescue.

Knowing it was the right call didn't make it any easier.

Now, with snow in the forecast, a generator overdue for inspection, six rooms full of guests expecting candy-cane cheer with an extra helping of holiday magic, and two impressionable daughters determined to play hostess without adult supervision, Graham felt the pressure mounting.

No backup.

No buffer.

No Margaret.

Just him.

It had been that way for years now.

He'd gotten used to it—used to the tightness in his chest every December, used to holding everything together with duct tape and grit because that's what you do when you're a single dad and the only thing standing between two little girls and the world. The to-do lists grew longer; the help became less reliable. The inn still looked like it did in the photos, wreaths hung on schedule, the cocoa bar was stocked, the reservation books were full...but it didn't feel the same. Not since Margaret.

Back then, Christmas felt magical. Holiday music drifted through the parlor as the aroma of sugar cookies filled the air. She'd hum softly while tying ribbons on the napkins. She'd sneak extra marshmallows into the kids' cups before they could even ask. And he'd watch her move—hair piled in a bun, mismatched socks but put together in a festive way—and think that maybe joy could exist in a place.

The first Christmas without her, he thought he could replicate it. He tried. Oh, how he tried. Graham hung every garland while the girls slept in their cradles. He ran the gingerbread activity as if his life depended on it, and it did. He burned the first three batches of cookies and forgot to set out the cocoa until Helen reminded him.

That first year had been held together with bandages and binding thread. The second was a bit easier because expectations had lowered. But nothing ever brought it back to the way it had been.

Until now.

Graham remained still, letting it unfold around him, unsure whether he should stop it or if he was witnessing some kind of miracle.

Because someone else had stepped in now.

Wearing a cardigan dusted with flour and that quiet, calm command he hadn't realized he missed. Jess moved through the house like she'd always belonged—her voice warm, steady, delivering instructions with a smile that never made you feel bossed around. She didn't direct from afar. She crouched at eye level with Clara and listened when Noelle.

Graham didn't like messes. Not literal ones, and certainly not the emotional kind that came with remembering what it had been like—before. When the girls were too young to ask why they didn't have a mom or why he was the only one there to help them write their holiday wish lists.

He grabbed the flashlight from the shelf and clicked it on. The beam was strong. Good.

Satisfied, he climbed the basement stairs and crossed the hallway into the kitchen. Light shone through the frosted window above the sink. Cinnamon and a sugary scent filled the air. Jess, again.

She never seemed to stay in one place for long. Some women filled a room with perfume or chatter—Jess filled it with movement. She'd helped to string lights that morning as if it were nothing. Even Helen and her narcoleptic husband had been more animated since Jess arrived. There was stillness on the ridge while the storm was brewing, but today the inn felt...uplifted.

He stepped onto the back stoop to check the propane tanks but paused when he heard her humming under her breath "Let It Snow." Probably didn't even realize she was doing it. He stared out at the ridge and blinked against the cold.

Margaret used to do that. She'd break into holiday songs and forget that anyone else could hear her. Warmth fluttered somewhere behind his ribs and he tried to ignore it.

Instead, he busied himself turning the knobs and checking valves. By the time he stepped back inside, Jess was gone—probably off refilling cocoa or building a marshmallow village.

In the parlor, the day's activities were written on the chalkboard in a neat, cheerful script. Even the handwriting had improved.

The inn wasn't exactly running without him—but it wasn't running only because of him either.

That scared the hell out of him.

He'd held the reins so tightly for so long that he didn't know how to let go. But seeing the girls shine brighter around Jess and hearing their giggles echo through the old house—it was undeniable.

They didn't just need a dad.

They needed more joy. More chaos. More gingerbread dance floors and cotton-ball clouds that doubled as snow piles. They needed someone who wasn't still afraid that the mess of memories they had locked away might just break free.

They needed someone unafraid to make new memories, even if the old ones still hurt.

And Jess?

She seemed to be doing that by accident.

He found her again that afternoon, crouched on the front porch next to Clara, carefully overseeing the placement of fresh garland. Jess held a ball of twine in one hand, a mug of cocoa in the other, and had her hair pulled half-up with a pen she must've borrowed from the guest book station.

"You two good out here?" he asked, folding his arms against the porch post.

Clara gave a thumbs-up without looking away from her work.

"You're witnessing the birth of a holiday hedge masterpiece," Jess said, turning to him with a smile that hit harder than it should've. "No pressure, but we might need street-facing approval before we go full North Pole."

He blinked, deadpan. "Clara handles all decorative approvals for the HOA. I just work here."

Jess stood and faced him head-on, brushing off her knees. "We made emotional support cookies. Anything else you need? Locate the first aid kit? Deploy an emergency cocoa station?"

His throat tightened. Humor helped. "You run kitchens this well at your clinic?"

She smiled. "Not unless you count making drip coffee, refilling the vending machine, or talking a nurse down from murder after someone leaves the pot empty. Again."

His laugh was soft and genuine. Something about it eased the tension he'd been carrying all week.

Then she looked at him—really looked—and everything stopped. The cold bit at his ears, but he couldn't quite bring himself to move.

"Storm's gonna get worse before it gets better," he said softly.

Jess nodded. "I heard. Guess this Christmas will come with a snowman guarantee."

His voice softened. "If you want to pack early, I get it. Could help with—"

I'm not going," Jess interrupted. "Unless you kick me out.

Their gazes caught.

He saw what she was made of then—not bravado, not over-confidence—but steadfastness.

Maybe he wasn't the only one still learning how to stay when things got messy.

"I won't," he said.

She nodded once. A beat passed.

"We still have another day, maybe two, to prep," he said, voice fraying a little at the edges. "Thanks for making sure things keep running inside. And...for what you've done with the girls."

Her gaze softened. "Mostly just here to fend off icing-induced diabetes and craft-related injuries."

He smiled just a little and turned back toward the door.

Not because he wanted to leave.

But because he wasn't sure what he'd say if he stayed.

Chapter Eight

Jessica

The fire in the parlor crackled softly, casting a gentle glow across the knotty pine floors and quilts casually draped over the armchairs.

Jess shifted on the couch, her knees tucked up beneath her and her hands wrapped around a cup of cocoa too decadent to be good for anything but soothing one's senses. Homemade marshmallows floated on top, melting slowly. Clara had insisted on toasting them "just a little," and now the room smelled like sugar and nostalgia.

Clara sat cross-legged on the rug in front of the hearth, carefully sorting puzzle pieces into the lid of the box. She wore plaid flannel pajamas and a determined expression that seemed more grown-up than her single-digit years should allow.

Noelle, meanwhile, sprawled upside down in one of the wingback chairs, her legs hanging over an armrest, her hair fallen to the floor in messy braids, and she had a candy cane seemingly glued between her fingers.

"I think the fireplace makes the cocoa better," Noelle said, her voice muffled by marshmallow. "It's science."

"That's not science. Science isn't about how things make you feel," Clara said flatly, not looking up.

"It's the other science."

"There's only one science."

"Well, actually—never mind." Clara said, as Jess smiled into her mug, letting their banter wash over her like a holiday soundtrack.

"Do you always decorate the cocoa?" Jess asked them. "Peppermint spoons, whipped cream towers, mini gingerbread cookies balanced on the rim?"

Noelle sat up slowly, stray hair sticking out in wild directions. "Mama loved it. One special, any which way you like it, cocoa night. Dad says it's too much, but—"

Clara added, "But it's tradition. Grandma says he can 'like it or love it.' She helps buy all the stuff every year. I think he deep down inside loves it."

"Fair," Jess murmured.

The room was quiet and peaceful, just like the calm at the end of a long day at dusk. Outside, the storm was gathering with increasing strength. The wind softly rattled the windowpanes but hadn't yet become fierce. Graham had said they probably had until morning—and then it would turn.

Jess sipped her cocoa and stretched her legs.

The twins' bedtime was an hour away, and she had already promised to help Clara with her new knit stocking kit tomorrow. Noelle had asked if she could read them The Night Before Christmas at bedtime. Jess had agreed without hesitation. She hadn't planned on getting this attached.

She hadn't planned on any of this.

Graham's voice broke into her thoughts.

"Everything okay in here?"

He stood in the archway just beyond the parlor, arms loosely folded, still wearing the flannel jacket he hadn't taken off, with a quiet look in his eyes that made Jess sit up a little straighter. He moved through the house like those old rescue dogs with barrels around their necks—always circling, always watching. Always on alert. He stayed on the edges, making sure everything went smoothly. But did he ever pause long enough to enjoy the warmth he worked so hard to protect?

"We're fine," she said. "Just hanging out and drinking cocoa."

Clara nodded. "Noelle added extra marshmallows."

"Only because I had to!" Noelle said. "They were all stuck together."

Jess snorted. "Clearly she couldn't help it."

Graham stepped farther in, unwinding his scarf. His hair was tousled—not from vanity, but from use—curling in tendrils and dusted with melting snow like a man who'd worked a little too hard and needed a break.

"You look cold," Jess said softly as he walked by.

"You look...warm," he replied, then immediately seemed to regret saying it.

Jess blinked once, then raised an eyebrow.

"I'll be in the kitchen," Graham said abruptly, but his lips crooked upward before he turned. "Leave that puzzle half-finished, and I'll think less of all of you."

When the fire crackled again and the room quieted, Clara peeked up from the floor. "He's smiling more."

Jess swallowed. "I noticed."

Noelle slipped off the chair and flopped bonelessly beside her sister, candy cane still stuck to her hand.

"We have cookies for Santa," she announced. "And note, mine has glitter stickers, grandpa sent in our grocery delivery."

Clara gave him a thoughtful look. "Dad says Santa can't eat cookies with pecans. It makes his sleigh fly weird."

Jess blinked. "The logic in this house is fascinating."

"What do you mean?" asked Clara.

"Oh, nothing." Jess sipped her cocoa, the corners of her mouth curling up. He might not like pecans, but he clearly knows how to keep the holiday magic alive.

Later, after the girls finished their puzzle and trotted off to bed with a story and promises of marshmallow towers and sugar plum dreams, Jess stayed in the parlor and relit the fire. The wood snapped as it caught a spark, then settled low and steady.

Graham reappeared at the door.

"They're out for the count," he said. "Clara promised to build a realistic igloo once it snows, and Noelle asked if I could make glitter paint for the interior."

Jess smiled from where she knelt by the fireplace. "Did you say yes?"

"I said I'd consider it. That kid does not need another way to utilize glitter." He stepped forward, watching as she added one more log to the flame. "But she'll find a way to make it, regardless."

"She's resourceful."

He tilted his head. "So, are you."

Jess turned, slowly rising to her full height and brushing ash off her fingers. "That a compliment?"

He shrugged one shoulder. "Just calling it like I see it."

A beat stretched between them.

Jess studied his face—the exhaustion in his shoulders, the careful tension in his jaw, and that steady kind of focus he wore like a second flannel. She saw the steel in him, the way it never looked flashy, just necessary. Deliberate. There was resolve in his eyes, and a quiet ache hidden behind it—tightly sealed, but there. She'd stopped pretending she couldn't see it.

He wasn't one to show vulnerability: no big declarations or emotional scenes. But in the soft glow of firelight and the way his fingertips hovered near the doorknob, she saw glimpses in the margins, the faintest signs of someone doing everything they can to keep their life together. He stayed near the exit, present but always ready to run, as his reality hit him.

He worked as if he believed all the responsibilities of the inn were solely on his shoulders. Maybe they were, when he was alone, but what surprised her—what truly stopped her—was how much the inn was thriving despite everything that had been lost.

The girls weren't just cared for; they were full of joy. Noelle, wild and unfiltered, sparkled like a little winter star. Clara, serious-eyed and cautious, was already a second set of boots walking beside him with too much awareness for her age.

Despite the good, Jess hadn't missed the bad—the way Clara took ownership of tasks not meant for an eight-year-old. How she read emotion like a language and smoothed edges before they turned sharp. She was holding the world together, one grip of perfection at a time. And Noelle? She was sprinting in the opposite direction, trailblazing chaos, measuring safety in laughter, sugar, and the exact right number of sparkles on a glue stick.

They might not have a mother, but their dad had clearly filled the void she left behind. Jess felt it like a thrum in her chest. They were growing around it, not through it, and Graham—

He kept everything moving, hardly stopping long enough to breathe.

"You okay?" she asked softly.

He nodded once, eyes flicking toward the hall. But his voice was tense. "Yeah."

Jess turned carefully to avoid crowding him and reached for the cocoa pot sitting on the warming tray near the bookshelf. She glanced over her shoulder. "The girls implied you liked your cocoa simple."

His brow twitched, surprised. "I do."

"No glitter marshmallows. No peppermint dust," she added, pouring into a sturdy ceramic mug. "No garnish. Just warm."

She handed it to him.

Their hands brushed briefly.

She stayed beside him even after he took a sip, watching the way he exhaled into the steam. He didn't relax—not completely—but she could feel the shift, the tension loosening by a thread.

He murmured, "You're good at this."

Jess raised a brow. "Handing over cocoa?"

"Making things easier."

His words hit a spot she'd been carefully ignoring. She swallowed and looked away slightly to hide the truth. She wasn't really trying to fix anything—at least not now—but this place had started to surround her quietly and unexpectedly. The girls. The house. Maybe him, too. She didn't realize she was craving any of it—until now. And once she felt it, helping became instinct, not a choice.

She smiled, tucking her hands into the sleeves of her cardigan. "Well...I'm a doctor. Care and preventative medicine are kind of my thing."

He gave her a look that said, *all right, doctor*—then took another sip.

Maybe it was the sugar-scented air, or the comfort in the gentle clinking of mugs in the background. Or maybe it was the fact that he was standing there looking so solid in that flannel, as if warmth didn't just cling to him but radiated from somewhere deeper. But Jess's thoughts wandered.

There were certainly other ways to warm him up.

The thought flickered hot and uninvited.

She looked away, her brows lifted just enough to tease. "I mean, if all your hard work isn't enough, we might need to resort to sharing body heat. Strictly for emergency purposes, of course."

"Helen might object, but..." Graham turned toward her, one brow raised, his eyes shining with something warm and amused. "I'll keep that in mind," he said softly.

Jess blinked, then laughed softly—surprised, maybe, but pleased, definitely. By the time she turned away, the tension in her shoulders had melted away.

"They're lucky to have you," she said suddenly. "The girls."

He looked away. "I'm not always...enough."

Jess stepped closer, quiet but firm. "They laugh with you. They trust you. They tell me about traditions you kept because you wanted them to know she loved them."

Graham's jaw tightened. "They never met her."

The breath caught in her lungs, and for a moment, exhaling felt impossible. Then it all rushed out. She hesitated, searching for the right words, before finally offering the only truth that mattered.

You've made sure they know her every day. They might not have had time together, but when they think of her...they still know exactly who she was.

He nodded and stared into his cocoa as if it contained the secrets of the universe. "And you let them build candy dance floors, even when it drives you crazy."

That drew a laugh from him. Quiet but real.

"They're better because of you," Jess said. "And that matters more than perfect braids or sticking to the rules."

He met her gaze, something shifting slowly and subtly.

"You're not what I expected when you showed up here," he said roughly.

"Because I wore heels?"

"Because you stayed."

She waited, then said, "I needed to be here, maybe as much as you've needed me."

That silenced both of them.

Wind gusted against the window. The fire popped to fill the

gap. Jess didn't move. Graham didn't either.

His voice was low as he said, "Storm's really coming this time. We'll probably lose power by midday tomorrow. You sure you still want to wait it out?"

Jess nodded. "We've got plenty of cocoa, and Noelle has squirreled away no less than three pounds of glitter in various places around this inn. What else could we need?"

His mouth twisted. "You sure?"

"I'm a doctor," she said casually. "I've survived worse. Plus, I have no doubt you've taken every precaution to ensure we're all safe and comfortable."

He smiled then—small, almost secret—but didn't look away.

They were too close now. No one else was in the room. No one else in the house was awake. There was nothing left to clean, chaperone, or redirect. Just this moment.

Jess took a step back as her heart raced.

"I made sure there were extra blankets in the parlor," she murmured. "In case the rooms get cold tomorrow night."

He nodded, his voice hoarse. "Thank you."

Jess began to leave, but Graham's voice stopped her again. "Jess?"

She paused.

He looked at her—no walls, no armor, no justifications.

"Thank you. For more than serving food and leading crafts," he said. "For making this house feel full again."

Jess didn't answer.

She just nodded, turned toward the stairs, and smiled the whole way up.

Chapter Nine

Graham

Outside, the first crystals of snow had drifted down onto the inn—light, lazy, and slow. Pine trees near the top of the ridge wore the beginnings of a powder coat, not yet heavy, but promising.

In the kitchen, Graham stood at the farmhouse sink, watching the snow begin to blur and soften the sharp features of Holly Ridge. His hands grasped a chipped blue mug, the coffee cold and untouched. He didn't drink it. He simply held it, palms around something to ground him in the moment. His expression was unreadable, but his shoulders remained still—squared yet relaxed—like a man savoring five more seconds before life required something from him again.

The snowfall wasn't dangerous at this point. That was the unsettling part.

It was the sort of snow people romanticized—a postcard layer, glowing bright white where the sun brushed an open stretch of ground. It clung weightless to the porch railings, tucked itself into the windowpanes, and wrapped every tree limb in frosted lines. Beautiful as all hell.

Too beautiful.

Because here, when it started soft and slow like this, Graham knew what came next. Inch by inch, it would thicken. Curl heavier. Slip wet into the eaves and weigh down the cedar branches until they bowed too far. If the temperature dipped just a little more, the snow would grip rather than dust. The phone lines might sag. The generator would groan. The inn would creak in the places it wasn't supposed to creak.

But for now...

He closed his eyes for a second.

For now, the world was hushed and glowing in snow-lit stillness.

From upstairs, small feet thudded across the floorboards, one a beat and a half behind. Jess's light laugh followed, muffled, echoing down the hallway along with the sleepy sounds of twin chatter. They were probably headed toward pancakes in the sunroom, which would be almost unbearably bright this morning. He knew the girls would have already started their snowmen lineup before their boots even hit the floor.

Graham let the moment stretch.

Another gust came across the ridge, brushing a billowing cloud of sharp, glittering ice against the side of the house with a soft hiss of pine needles skipping across shingles. He watched one branch tap against the kitchen window—more of a greeting than a warning.

"Daddy!"

Noelle's voice rang around the corner behind him. He

turned and crouched instinctively just as she rounded the table and threw herself at him with all her barefooted might.

"It's SNOW," she announced, as if his window view hadn't made that clear. "Like real snow, like the movie kind. IT'S STICKING."

Graham grunted under the weight of her hug and leaned back just enough to catch a piece of glitter stuck to the hem of her pajama shirt.

"Snow doesn't mean you don't need socks," he said lightly, brushing her cold ankle. "And it definitely doesn't mean we skip breakfast."

"But it's real right now," Noelle said dramatically, pointing toward the back door.

From behind her, Clara entered at a much more dignified pace, her robe tightly belted, and her hair already braided. "We checked the porch," she reported, like a scientist approaching the lab with findings. "Measurable coverage confirmed. At least half an inch, with more expected to fall. It's going to be a snow day!"

Graham nodded. "Not if you don't eat your eggs."

"Eggs are slimy," Noelle muttered.

"Eggs are fuel for snowman building," he replied.

Behind him, Jess's voice drifted in from the hallway, cheerful and unbothered. "I already started the cocoa. If we bribe them, it buys us ten extra minutes of cooperation."

Both girls gasped in excited unison.

Graham arched an eyebrow toward the counter as she entered. There was flour already on the sleeve of her cardigan. He couldn't tell if it was new or leftover from yesterday.

"More cocoa?" he asked dryly.

"I believe the official term is 'cold management beverage,'" she said, reaching past him to refill the kettle.

He held his ground.

For another minute, the snow danced outside the window like something magical, and his kitchen echoed with footsteps, warmth, and more love than logic.

It would get harder later.

But for now, it was beautiful.

The radio crackled loudly on the windowsill.

...and if you're heading north from Canyon or east past Pampa, roads are being monitored and are likely to be closed in both directions later today. Stay indoors and stay safe. Power crews are already working along the outer belt—authorities remind owners to keep driveways in the ridge communities clear, so emergency vehicles aren't blocked by snowfall...

He turned the volume down.

The storm had arrived.

They were prepared on the ridge. They might be isolated, but the propane heaters were running, the generator on top of the well house was still ticking along, and the flashlight drawer in the kitchen was stocked with batteries.

Graham had done everything he possibly could.

Now came the part he hated most—the waiting.

Jess crossed the kitchen to stand beside him. "You holding up okay?"

Graham nodded. "It's snowing."

I don't remember the last time I saw snow like this...we don't get it often near Houston. This much snow would have already shut down the city.

The corners of his mouth pulled. "Wouldn't be surprised if the inn loses power later. Then we'll be counting on the generator to keep the fridge cold and the heater running."

"Then we better start prepping," she replied, already assessing the room like she did during a town clinic flu surge. Sharp eyes, warm hands, calm demeanor. She moved like someone who'd handled worse and made everything feel less like a disaster and more like an inevitability.

By noon, the snowfall had doubled.

The road down Holly Ridge was buried beneath sculpted ribbons of snow, the wind curling and drifting it as if it couldn't decide where to land. Graham stood beside the wide sunroom windows, arms crossed tightly, watching the ridge disappear inch by cautious inch. From this height, the view usually calmed him—a stretch of quiet pine and open valley. But today, it looked like a holiday postcard: serene and still, with a lull of a winter wonderland masking the danger underneath.

Helen stood beside him, half-wrapped in an oversized sweater with a mug clasped in both hands, giving play-by-play updates as if she were broadcasting live from the weather desk.

"Well," she said, drawing out the word as if it needed room to breathe. "That's the second big wind gust followed by a heavier wave of snow. I thought I heard a motor a little while ago—maybe the snowplows are trying to keep the road open."

Graham's jaw was clenched, and he shifted slightly toward

the door, as if standing ready could keep the storm away.

"No one's coming up the ridge today," Helen said more softly. "Not unless they're airlifted."

Laughter erupted through the thick glass. Graham's eyes shifted to the main lawn. The twins were caked in powder from their boots to their beanies.

Clara lay on her back in the snow, eyes narrowed, lips pressed into a concentration that would typically be reserved for brain surgery or applying super glue without collateral damage. Her arms moved in stiff arcs; each motion deliberate and measured. Graham noticed her murmuring under her breath as she worked—probably counting strokes.

A puff of snow burst up around her boot as she adjusted the angle.

Not far off, Noelle had repurposed a plastic Tupperware container from the inn's kitchen and was steadily filling it with snow, packing it down with stubborn determination. Block after block, she'd packed and stacked, resulting in a lumpy-looking igloo. She'd attempted corners, curvature, and a peaked dome that had collapsed twice already. And now, judging by the uneven mound slowly taking shape beside her, she was committed to letting architectural consistency become someone else's concern.

He smiled despite himself.

The girls were themselves today. Loud. Demanding. Deep inside, there was something that wasn't grief, nostalgia, or anything touched by sorrow. It was just snow and warm breath.

Graham pressed his hand against the cold glass. "They've been out there twenty minutes."

Helen sipped her tea. "Uh huh."

It's wet. Noelle's not wearing two layers. Clara's already soaked through her socks. They'll freeze before long."

"They're learning something," she said, as Noelle slid across the crowded path on her belly, cackling the whole way. Clara followed seconds later and landed with a thud. "Looks like joy to me."

Graham shot her a sideways glance. "You ever get frostbite from joy, Helen?"

"Can't recall," she said pleasantly. "But I guess you could always change their socks and send them back out."

Outside, Clara stood tall, arms akimbo, and theatrically gestured toward the wind. Noelle waved a stick in the air as if casting spells.

He should call them in. It would be the smart, parental thing to do. The safe thing.

But they were laughing too hard.

And then he saw Jess, rounding the porch with her scarf pulled low, grinning so big it tugged something loose in his ribs. She jumped into the chaos like she belonged there. Clara handed her a mitten full of snow and immediately called her "The Snow Queen." Jess dropped into a deep curtsy, crowned herself with an upside-down bowl dusted with snow, and proclaimed the new law of the land: "Everyone shall eat cookies after battle!"

The girls howled.

He felt it again—that pull. The press of something more substantial than comfort. It wasn't an obligation or routine, but something warmer. A want.

"They've never played like this in the snow," he murmured.

Helen looked at him over her mug. "Maybe they've never had someone show them how."

He knew she meant Jess. He didn't need to ask.

Outside, Clara tackled Jess into a snow drift. Jess dramatically surrendered, hands thrown up as Noelle piled marshmallow-sized handfuls on her like a snow tribute. None of them looked anxious. None of them looked cold.

He hadn't realized how often he watched for signs of breakage—slipping, failing to hold the pieces together.

Now all the pieces were flying—and somehow, none of them were falling apart.

He exhaled through his nose and reached for his coat on the hook by the door.

"Where are you going?" Helen asked.

He didn't hesitate. "Out. Just to check on them."

Helen smiled faintly. "I'll have cookies ready. Apparently, it is a law. They'll need them after battle."

As he stepped outside, the cold slapped him in the face with the sharp serenity of real winter. The kind that talked back in the silence. That reminded you that a storm wasn't just danger—it could be wonder, too.

He planted his boots on the snow-covered porch steps and watched as Noelle handed Jess her snow wand with regal ceremony.

"She's gonna be soaked through," he muttered, brushing frost off the railing and shoving his hands into his coat pockets.

But Jess turned toward him just then, and her smile reached all the way to her eyes. She mouthed something he couldn't hear.

They're okay.

And he believed her. He let wonder be louder than worry, and, just for a little longer, he would just let them play.

Chapter Ten

Graham

All morning, he had pretended not to notice when Clara's tightly rolled snowballs turned into a full-blown ambush, or when Noelle started painting her igloo like a rainbow with water dyed with food coloring. Jess had been right there with them—laughing, flinging snow, and sinking knee-deep into drifts as if she had lived on the ridge forever.

From the wood pile, his gloved hands full of kindling, Graham watched them play. He'd been tempted to put down the ax and join in, but each hour brought the worst part of the storm closer. When the wind began to bite and whip through the trees, he sent the girls inside. The clouds above Holly House had turned iron gray, and flurries were thickening into heavier clumps of snow.

Eventually, the weather drove him inside as well. He found the girls warm and dry in their pajamas. Jess had her curls loosely braided and was partly perched on a stepladder in the front hall, a paper garland draped around her shoulder like a beauty queen's sash. The whole project was gloriously ridiculous. There were twenty feet of classic paper rings in white, blue, and glittering silver, with large glittery snowflakes at both ends. Flickering candles added ambiance—and were ready if the power went out. The Christmas tree with white lights flickered in the corner of the foyer, and the chain was hanging across the arched entryway, greeting guests into the parlor.

She made it all look absolutely perfect.

From the parlor, a holiday playlist drifted in—muffled crooners and soft jazz. Graham could hear the clatter of measuring cups in the kitchen, and the twins darted in and out like exuberant reindeer in socks.

He knew the checklist he'd left on the kitchen counter was incomplete. The breakfast room still needed firewood. He hadn't checked the hen house a second time or called the girls' grandparents. But instead of rushing back out the side door, Graham paused in the hallway, leaning his shoulder against the archway just long enough to watch Jess stretch upward, trying to fasten the end of the paper chain to a brass hook above the crown molding.

She grimaced and repositioned herself. Too far. "Don' t move," he said softly but firmly, stepping forward just as the ladder wobbled beneath her shifting weight.

Jess jumped in surprise. Her arms flailed as she reached out for an unseen hook. She yelped once—then Graham's hands appeared at her waist, catching her before she fell backward into a pile of paper rings.

They froze—shoulder to chest, his hands still gripping her. His mind went blank. The feel of her was unfamiliar and yet sparked cravings that were all too familiar.

Jess looked up.

They were too close—definitely too close—his palms splayed across her ribcage, her breath warm against his collar.

"Hi," she muttered, a startled smile tugging at her lips.

Graham didn't move. Couldn't.

Her eyes were wide with adrenaline but not fear—surprise, something softer. Her whole body buzzed with it, which, unfortunately, mirrored exactly how he felt, like the charge of a storm just before a lightning strike.

"I said don't move," he said, one brow lifting.

"Well." She smiled, still breathless. "It's a little late for that."

He didn't smile back. He couldn't, not with the blood pounding in his ears, but he didn't look away either. Not until her hand gently brushed along his wrist, just enough to remind him they were still touching.

Jess cleared her throat. "You can let go now."

Right. He stepped back. Too fast. She looked flushed. In the wake of their closeness, the hallway felt too loud with silence.

The ladder wobbled as she climbed back up and reached again, this time victorious. The garland draped down, shimmering softly.

Graham exhaled and nodded, short and gruff. "That's good. It's festive."

Jess eyed him. "You mean 'glamorous with a side of grade-school charm.'"

"It suits the inn," he said—and meant it.

Somewhere behind them, Noelle shrieked with joy. Clara thundered down the stairs holding a stack of snowflake cutouts like armor. Jess laughed, voice low, chest still rising a little too fast.

He left her perched on the ladder and ducked into the parlor. There was salt left to spread by the back door, along with the rest of his checklist. He was rushing to finish busy work, but he didn't miss the way her smile lingered even after he'd gone. It was as if something had shifted, but hadn't quite settled yet.

By the time Graham returned an hour later, the inn glowed.

The tree had been redecorated with homemade cranberry strings and popcorn garland. A decorated box filled with jingle bells sat near the guest register, and someone had turned on the small plastic lantern by the coat hooks. Its flickering digital flame emitted a charming, yet unnecessary, light.

Graham didn't know how Jess managed it all without a battalion of elves. But the place looked radiant.

At the dining table, Noelle was trying to open the fancy, folded Christmas crowns for the place settings, each one shaped like a different winter animal. "Mine looks like a hedgehog," she announced proudly. Jess leaned in to help her fix the tab in place.

Clara finished looping a silver ribbon around a tray of cards labeled 'Holiday Trivia—Round 1,' her handwriting precise and her expression focused. It seemed like the success of dinner depended on the spacing between categories and bonus points.

Aw, she had recruited his gang of holiday helpers.

And somehow, they worked better for her than they ever

had for him.

He leaned against the archway just long enough to take it all in: the soft hum of silver against plates, the pink-cheeked buzz of families choosing seats, and the quiet grace with which Jess stepped into a dozen roles without missing a beat. Graham felt both amazed and slightly irrelevant in the best, most disorienting way.

Helen and her husband claimed the window table, with wool scarves hanging from the backs of their chairs. She gently patted his hand while balancing her knitting on her lap. He looked blissful, like a man handed a warm plate and a generous pour of spiked cider. Helen clearly had been conspiring with Jess. She knew all the Holly House traditions. When she handed out her hand-stitched holiday napkins—each adorned with a tiny red bow—Graham could swear the woman glowed.

The small family who had played in the snow earlier had just taken a table near the fire. Their daughter had increased her glitter use and still had flecks on her from earlier crafting—despite her mother's efforts with a damp cloth. The toddler squealed at the bell hidden in his napkin ring, prompting chuckles and subtle trades for more toddler-safe accessories. It was the kind of chaos Margaret thrived on.

Tonight, God help them all—Margaret would be proud.

Jess approached him with a bundle of folded trivia answer sheets and a spark in her eye that made his brain short-circuit for half a second.

"Don't take this the wrong way," he said, "but you've set the bar dangerously high. Tomorrow's Christmas Eve. We'll never top this."

She raised an eyebrow, all steady confidence, like she was explaining post-op instructions. "I don't need to top it," she said, offering him a clipboard. "Tomorrow has its own magic. Christmas Eve is special all by itself: hanging stockings, cookies for Santa, and the anticipation. But tonight..." She glanced over her shoulder at the guests settling in, laughter bubbling up. "Tonight, we're well-lit, well-fed, and we've got time before the power decides to test us. Make hay while the sun is shining."

"Or before the generator starts humming," he said, amused.

Jess grinned. "Exactly."

He nodded softly, taking it in. She just walked into a place and made it warmer.

He had wondered, now and then, if the house could ever feel the way it used to—alive, lit from the inside out—not just functional, but full. Watching Clara smooth the edge of her trivia cards, Noelle toss marshmallows into the air, and Helen smiled at her husband as she twined their fingers like newlyweds. He realized, with deep clarity in the place where fear used to sit, the house didn't just feel alive tonight. It felt whole.

And he knew, with absolute certainty, why.

"Okay!" Jess called from the head of the dining table, standing between a scattered stack of trivia cards, a clipboard, and a crystal bowl full of peppermint candies that had somehow become the official prize currency. She tapped a spoon against her glass, prompting half the table to groan in playful protest.

"Time for another round," she announced with the

mock-seriousness of a game show host. "Winner gets bragging rights, one free marshmallow of their choice tomorrow morning, and—courtesy of Noelle—a golden pinecone she found behind the woodshed."

"I glittered it!" Noelle added, holding it aloft like a sacred artifact.

Graham leaned a shoulder into the doorframe, arms crossed, with one boot cocked against the threshold. His girls were at the table—Noelle practically vibrating, Clara using her sleeve to line up her pen with military precision—both glowing from the inside out.

Jess cleared her throat and read aloud, "Which reindeer is named last in the original poem *A Visit from St. Nicholas*—more commonly known as *'Twas the Night Before Christmas*?"

A low ripple of muttering spread across the group.

"Blitzen?"

"No, no—it's Donner!"

"Is Rudolph even in that poem?"

Jess grinned. "Five seconds."

Someone called out "Vixen," only to be booed by half the room.

"It's Cupid!" Clara said quickly, pressing her pen down like she was locking in a game show answer.

Jess looked toward her with mock solemnity, then flipped the card.

"Correct!" She tossed a peppermint into Clara's pile with cheerful flair.

"Next question," she said, pulling another card. "This one's a speed round. Bonus candy for whoever finishes first. What is Frosty's nose made of?"

Noelle's hand shot up like she was in school. "A carrot!"

"Close," Jess said, stifling a laugh. "What is the song? *Frosty the Snowman...*"

"Was a jolly, happy soul!" Clara sang, then the rest of the table joined in: "With a corn cob pipe, and a—"

"Button nose!" Noelle finished triumphantly.

The laughter came easily after that—some loud, some soft and tired, but all real.

Graham stood in the shadowed hallway. He watched for a moment the arc of Jess's hand, the way she laughed, the sparkle in his daughters' eyes—and the way the inn didn't just survive around her.

It expanded. It breathed, and for the first time in a long, long while...so did he.

After dinner, Jess waved him in from the hall. "They're gearing up for charades," she warned, eyes bright. "Apparently, Helen's been undefeated since 2017."

Graham squinted toward the parlor. "That tracks."

Jess nudged a paper snowman wreath onto his arm. "You're Team Frosty."

"Hard pass."

"You don't even know the rules."

"I know enough."

The paper wreath slipped off his arm and fell to his feet. He turned just enough to see Jess watching him with a smile that didn't quite seem smug. He wasn't sure if he wanted to escape it—or stay there forever.

She leaned in—not too close, but close enough. "You're stalling because you know we'll destroy you."

"Charades is not a sanctioned holiday competition."

"Maybe not," she said, picking up the wreath again. Her fingers brushed his. "But Helen's really hoping if she gets it going this year, it'll be added as an official Holly House tradition next year."

"That woman is a schemer."

"True, and unapologetic."

Graham looked into the parlor where the guests were gathered. Light shone through the trimmed window panes. Laughter filled the room, along with the creak of old chairs and the sound of Clara's giggles weaving beneath Noelle's dramatic impression of Santa Claus.

The house had never been more alive.

Jess smiled at him, tilting her chin up. "Join us. It will be fun."

Somehow...he believed her.

He nodded and stepped through the archway and into the light.

Chapter Eleven

Jessica

She woke early the next morning, not because anything had specifically woken her, but because the silence outside her door had grown deeper. It was the kind of quiet that suggested something had shifted overnight. Now, snuggled in her bed, she could hear how the wind caused the rafters to creak softly, as the Holly House adjusted to the gusts and the weight of the falling snow.

Reluctantly, she pushed back the thick quilt and slipped into her slippers to quietly descend the stairs toward the sunroom. The house and everyone inside remained quiet and asleep—probably lulled by the complete silence. There were no voices, no fans, no buzzing light bulbs. Holly House had lost power overnight.

She paused, listening to the faint hum of the generator. Nothing. Was Graham still asleep as well?

Her steps softened as she moved across the pine floorboards. Noelle's drawing of a snow woman—stick-armed, marshmallow-crowned, and proudly labeled QUEEN COCOA in pink glitter pen—still hung beside the cocoa bar. Jess smiled and gently straightened the crooked corner.

The kitchen was empty. The stove was cold. But the air still carried a trace of cinnamon and coffee.

She flipped the light switch out of habit. Nothing.

Of course.

The storm hadn't howled, nor was there a dramatic crash of ice in the gutters. It was simply a quiet, matter-of-fact blackout, as if the house had blinked and let go.

The teapot on the stove caught her eye. She knew how to light the burner manually, but her gaze settled on a jar of instant coffee near the industrial brewer. A dirty spoon lay nearby on a paper towel. The teapot was warm.

"I guess I'm not the first one up," she murmured.

She grabbed a flashlight and headed to the pantry. Graham had already done his pre-storm checks—twice—but she still needed a plan. Bread. Peanut butter. Clara's neatly labeled cocoa mixes lined one shelf. Jess smiled again.

The kitchen was silent, only her and the steady ticking of the old wall clock in the corner. Dawn had just begun to cast its pale light through the frost-covered windowpanes.

Jess sliced into a soft loaf of white bread, the rhythmic motion soothing her nerves. There wasn't much to work with, not without power, but she managed to make it work. PB&Js stacked in careful triangles, fruit that hadn't quite gone warm, and a bowl of hard-boiled eggs from the back of the fridge. Functional. Thoughtful.

Then came a faint sound. It was metallic, steady, muffled.

She smiled. Mystery solved. Graham was in the basement workshop.

After pouring the last of the hot water from the kettle, she opened the jar of instant coffee. She guessed at the amount. He would want his coffee to be simple, strong, and without any frills. Black.

Like his cocoa. Nothing fancy, just simple and warm.

The stairs creaked as she descended, one hand steadying the mug. The air turned cooler downstairs, filled with the scent of wood and old tools. Around the last corner, she saw him. Graham had his jacket sleeves rolled up, grease smeared on his wrist, and he was leaning over a stubborn piece of machinery.

She stayed back, watching. His face wasn't angry, just focused. Worn.

"Morning," she said as she walked into the room.

The basement walls were made of aged cinderblock. One side lined with pantry overflow, and the other with tools and a long, well-used workbench.

Graham looked up, one hand bracing his knee, the other wiping his palm with a rag. "Did I wake you?"

"No. It's quiet upstairs, but people will start stirring soon," she said, offering the mug. "I figured you could use this."

His fingers brushed hers as he took the cup, the warmth shared between them.

"Thanks." He nodded and took a sip, quietly hissing when it was too hot, but he didn't complain.

Jess's gaze flicked to the dismantled parts on the bench. "Everything okay?"

I've been down here since four, trying to get this thing to

work. He exhaled slowly. It was fine yesterday, but this morning, nothing. I might've flooded the carburetor trying to stay ahead of the freeze, or it's the filter.

"So, you took it all apart and now you're putting it back together?"

"Something like that."

She sat on a nearby stool; her hands wrapped around her cooling tea. "Take your time. Breakfast is covered."

He turned just a bit. "You made breakfast?"

Yeah, it's not up to your usual Holly House standards. PB&Js, fruit, and some eggs. It's not glamorous, but hopefully it will be enough to keep people from eating each other.

That elicited a quiet chuckle from him, but he looked down into his mug again.

"The fridge is warming up," she added. "We should plan to eat what we can today, just in case you can't get the generator going."

"I should've been on that already." He nodded, slower now. "I'm hoping to get this fixed soon."

You've been working eighteen-hour days, hosting guests, parenting two cocoa-fueled kids, and preparing for a storm. Forgive yourself.

The silence that followed wasn't cold, just still.

"You're covering the stuff I usually handle," he said, fingers tightening around the warm mug as if it were the only solid thing in the room. "You're supposed to be enjoying a peaceful holiday."

"I wasn't raised with ingrained holiday traditions," Jess glanced at him, her palms pressed flat on the workbench. "Honestly, I'm happy to help. I've gotten good at taking care of the stuff. You know...paperwork, logistics, paperwork about logistics."

A brief flicker of a smile crossed his face. It didn't stay, but it appeared. A quick glimmer.

Yeah," he murmured. "I imagine running a medical clinic is more difficult than running an inn. I mean, I have to worry about power, breakfast, and whether someone is going to try to steal the cloth napkins, but your work—you have to make sure people don't die.

Jess exhaled slowly, pressing her fingers against the generator casing. She usually didn't talk about this part—not in detail, and only if someone asked, which rarely happened.

"There are days..." she began, eyes distant with a tiredness that no amount of sleep could fix.

There are days when the clinic feels like a dozen ticking clocks. A mother clutching her feverish child at 9:02 a.m., a teenager with a panic attack at 10:17 a.m., a husband trying not to cry because his wife's biopsy results came back while he was refilling the coffee at 11:41 a.m. It is never just the medicine; it is the whole weight of someone else's everything.

She paused, breath catching. "I love it. It's mine. But sometimes it is relentless. There is no room for sick days, birthday brunch, or silence. You wake up afraid of what is waiting. Not because you cannot handle it—because you always do—but because you've forgotten the last time you felt anything besides exhaustion."

Graham studied her, motionless.

"I used to think that if I just worked hard enough, I could

outrun the loneliness," Jess added. "Fill up every minute until the emptiness had nowhere to land, but I could nail a diagnosis in sixty seconds flat and still forget whether I had eaten that day. Somehow, I managed to help everyone...except myself."

The last words escaped more quietly than the rest. And maybe that was the truth behind it all—that she was completely exhausted from carrying the weight alone.

Graham's voice was quiet when he finally replied. "That sounds like hell, and I raised twins. I know tired."

Jess let out a laugh that didn't quite reach her eyes. "Some days are really bad, but other days? Those days you save someone. You hold their hand while they breathe through grief, you walk them back into the world, and, for a moment, it's all that matters."

He held her gaze for a beat longer, then looked away like her confession had knocked something loose.

"After Margaret passed..." he began slowly, words drawn from a deep part he rarely accessed, "I didn't just lose my wife. I lost every routine our life used to have."

He ran a hand across the back of his neck.

She shaped this place into something gentle and warm. She didn't need it to be perfect, just meaningful. Holiday napkins, toy bins in the closet for little guests, birthday candles hidden in the cabinet—just in case. After she died, I clung to the routines, thinking that if I could just keep the lights on and the hot cocoa warm, it might feel like she hadn't really left.

He looked down at the mug again. "Only, nothing's felt warm. Not for a long time."

Jess listened quietly, allowing those words to settle between them like the snow falling outside the back door.

"I didn't know what I was doing with the girls," Graham continued. "Hell, I didn't know what I was doing with myself. I spent so much time trying not to let anything fall apart that I forgot to check what should actually be standing. I kept everyone fed, patched the roof, and replaced the light bulbs. No one needed to ask or remind me, but I think...I forgot what it's like to stop, dig deep, and really want something."

Jess felt her throat tighten. "I've never been married. Never had kids. But I've burned through so many good people because I didn't know how to want more and still be who I am. Driven. Focused. Useful."

She swallowed and looked down at the oil-stained floor. "Sometimes I wonder if I'm built more for purpose than partnership."

He placed the coffee mug on the workbench, turning it slowly as if he was thinking over every possible thing to say next.

And sometimes," he murmured, "you find someone who makes partnership feel like purpose."

Jess looked up. Graham met her gaze with his—bare, unguarded.

That's what Margaret was for you," she said quietly.

"Yes." His voice roughened. "And I thought that was something I'd only get once. I believed lightning doesn't strike someone twice."

Jess leaned in carefully, not pushing. "Maybe it doesn't."

A pause.

"Maybe, love is a slower burn the second time."

Graham's breath hitched. Not a sob. Not from grief.

Something gentler. Surprise. Maybe hope.

Jess added softly, "These days with you...it hasn't felt like borrowed joy. There's something real here. I think you feel it, too."

He didn't speak, but his hand flexed against the corner of the worktable. She stayed still, giving him the space he needed.

"Jess," he said, voice low and rough-edged. "I wasn't expecting you."

She smiled quietly and honestly. "Neither was I."

Graham reached out for her hand, and she allowed him to take it.

He held her, squeezed her tightly, then exhaled slowly. "She wasn't a big woman," he said. "But she was strong. Carrying both girls wore her out more than she let on. Still, she hung every garland. Baked every cookie. Made crafts with the nieces like she had something to prove, or like she already knew it would be our last Christmas."

Jess didn't interrupt. Her fingers remained curled around his, steady. Present.

When the time came, they took the girls early. There were complications. Margaret was able to hold them, but only for a few moments.

Jess shut her eyes.

"I brought the twins home alone," he continued, the words more tired than broken. "Two car seats. No wife. No plan. I parked outside that door and just sat there for...I don't even know how long. I looked at this house and thought, how the hell do I make it feel like love still lives here?"

Jess watched him. Not with pity, she'd seen others fall apart when he stood up, but with something aching, fierce, and full of understanding.

Graham shook his head once. "It always felt like I was trying to do enough to keep her memory alive without spoiling everything else. The house, the girls, the inn...They all needed me, and I held on so tightly I forgot what normal looked like." He looked down into his coffee as if it might explain something, then said, "This is the first December since she passed that the house has felt warm. Alive. Like it was when she was here."

Gently, Jess took his mug and placed it beside the pile of tools. Then her fingers slid back into his.

"I didn't know her," she said. "But I see her everywhere: in your girls' joy, in how guests feel more at home here than anywhere else, and in the way this inn leans into the season like it still believes in wonder."

His eyes met hers. Vulnerable. Tired. Open.

"You've kept her magic going," Jess continued. "Even when it hurt. Even when it was hard. You built something good here, Graham, and you don't have to carry it all alone anymore."

He said nothing but didn't look away or move.

She laced their fingers together. "I'll help," she said, firm but gentle. "With the girls. We will make this special together, whether you planned for it or not."

Still nothing. Yet, every ounce of his expression had changed.

She squeezed his hand. "Come on, let's make this a Christmas the girls won't forget! For Helen. For everyone in this house. And," her voice softened, "for Margaret."

That's when he finally nodded—barely—but it was

enough.

Chapter Twelve

Jessica

Once everyone was awake, Holly House hummed with good-spirited cheer. The lack of power had not been a surprise, so the guests had emerged from their rooms bundled in cable-knit layers, thick slippers, and assorted combinations of fleece and flannel.

Jess greeted each guest with a warm smile, making sure everyone was settled in the parlor—the only room with a fire big enough to chase away the chill. Spirits were high, and the old walls held the heat for now, but the silence was starting to get to her. Without the usual hum of a busy house, Jess noticed every floorboard creak and the groan of the wind outside.

Determined to stay focused on making the best of a tough situation, she stood in the kitchen with her hair tied in a messy knot and sleeves rolled up to her elbows, directing her impromptu sous-chef team to help with breakfast. "Clara, triangle cuts for the sandwiches, please. Diagonals make it fancy."

Clara, standing on her step stool, nodded solemnly. Her

cuts were slow and precise, and she was clearly trying to cut the bread perfectly from corner to corner.

"And Noelle," Jess continued, pulling open a drawer for napkins, "you're in charge of making the fruit salad. We'll need at least half a cup per person. So, fill this up." She pushed a bowl across the kitchen island. "If I see glitter on anything, I'll make you eat a vegetable."

Noelle gasped dramatically. "You wouldn't!"

Jess handed her a spoon. "Try me."

In truth, Noelle was doing well—for a chaos goblin in fleece pajamas. Her station was sticky, but the fruit salad was bright and cheerful, and the eggs had made it from the fridge to the countertop safely.

The twin enthusiastic helpers carried everything to the parlor. Clara led the way with a platter of sandwiches, while Noelle announced the menu like a small-town auctioneer.

"PB&Js with crusts removed! Get 'em while they're still room temperature!"

Helen chuckled as she handed out mugs of hot water for tea and instant coffee. Guests spread out across the parlor, curled up in upholstered chairs or stretched out on couches in knit shawls and fleece throws. A few had moved toward the fire, where the flickering flames cast a jagged, uneven heat.

Someone hummed "Let It Snow." Jess heard the girls join in with more passion than pitch.

She leaned in the pantry doorway, taking in the scene: Noelle's fruit salad, decorated with cookie-cutter apple stars; Helen's husband trying to butter toast with stiff fingers; Clara crossing the rug, tray balanced in both hands like a pro.

It wasn't flashy—no French toast soufflés or truffled eggs—but it was warm. It was enough. And something about the whole patchwork moment, this homespun resilience—felt exactly right.

She checked the burner flame, adjusted it slightly lower, and placed a new kettle on to boil.

Then, once the trays were removed and the girls were too busy singing carols with the honeymoon couple to notice, Jess slipped down the back hallway toward the mudroom, phone in hand.

Her reception bars bounced between one and two. She paused briefly, then tapped the contact.

"Come on," she murmured. "Please pick up." The quiet press of anxiety she had been carrying all morning intensified.

After the third ring, a warm Southern drawl answered.

"Jess! I was just about to text you!"

"Candy." Jess exhaled, relief pooling in her limbs. "You all okay?"

I saw the weather reports. Y'all are gettin' way more snow than us," Candy replied. Pots clanged faintly in the background. "Power's blinking like a bad Vegas sign, but we're fine. The town's shut down. The bakery's dark. Bailey's up to her ears in chaos, trying to entertain Rosie, Mac, and that ridiculous goat, Mister Whatever Pants.

Jess smiled faintly and shifted the phone between her shoulder and cheek, tugging her cardigan closer. "Power is gone here. The generator's throwing a tantrum. Graham's been in the basement since dawn trying to charm it back to life with a wrench." She glanced toward the oven, already cold. "Meanwhile, I've cooked up a three-course breakfast of peanut butter, vaguely warm fruit, and hard-boiled eggs we're pretending are gourmet. The girls are impressed."

There was a pause, then the faint rustle of foil.

"Graham?" Candy repeated, over-enunciating. "The *innkeeper*?"

"Mmhmm."

"The same man you texted me about on day one as *'grumpy with an axe'*?"

"Well, technically, it's a chainsaw," Jess admitted. "But yes."

Another pause. Jess felt her smile betray her.

"And now he's just...Graham?" Candy teased.

Jess opened the pantry, mostly to have something to do with her hands. "He's still grumpy. Loves leaning on door frames to silently judge people. But he's also been panic-checking his 'to-do' list all day. He's given up sleep to prep for this storm, and all the while, he's keeping the guests stocked with gallons of cocoa. He's...steady."

"Jess," Candy said slowly, amusement thick in her voice. "Are you telling me you found your Hallmark Christmas hero? Snowstorm and all?"

A sigh. Jess rested her forehead against the pantry door. "He's not a tree farmer."

"No?"

"No. He's a widowed innkeeper with twin girls, a tool belt, and the emotional armor of someone who's seen his fair share of hurt, but..." she added, eyes drifting toward the sound of Clara and Noelle laughing in the parlor, "he's all the other things. The quiet, good ones."

"Well, butter my biscuit," Candy whispered. "Jess."

"I know."

"You like him."

Jess laughed, but it sounded a little hollow. "I do."

There was a creak on the other end—Candy settling into a chair, probably wiping her hands on one of her frayed holiday aprons.

"Is it hard?" she asked softly.

Jess paused. "Yeah. A little."

She wrapped an arm around her waist, pressing gently, as if to keep everything in place. "I came here for quiet. For space. Instead, I got two kids who believe I invented holiday magic, cocoa with more toppings than chocolate, and a man who watches silently and seems to see everything."

Candy made a gentle sound of understanding.

And are you prepared for that?

"I don't know," Jess whispered. "But I feel something...between the garlands and the storm and the way he looks at his girls. It's messy and warm and—when I'm there—it feels like being needed in a way that I don't even feel when saving lives at the clinic."

Silence.

Then—

"So...not a tree farmer," Candy said at last. "But better."

Jess smiled, thinking about it. "Yeah."

You want me to start clearing out your townhouse?

"I might never leave this ridge," Jess said honestly. Then, softer: "But don't toss the key just yet."

On the other end, Candy let out a laugh tinged with pride

and something more profound.

Okay, Doc. It sounds like the universe might have given you more than just cocoa and quiet this Christmas.

Jess tilted her head back, eyes closed. "Yeah. I think so."

"Well, for the record," Candy added, "I'm proud of you."

Jess blinked. "That is weirdly comforting. Thanks."

A pause, just long enough that Jess nearly checked the signal.

"Molly's at the hospital."

Jess straightened. "Wait—what?"

Her water broke this morning. Jackson called at five. Bailey is in full-on Mama Mode. She sent me to the bakery, packed a Ziplock as big as a pillowcase, and rushed off.

Despite the sting of sudden tears, Jess managed a smile. "So, today's the day?"

"Looks like it."

"Is she okay?"

Candy's voice softened. "So far, yes. It's early labor, but she's calm. Jackson's calm by proximity. They are lucky. But what kid *wants* a Christmas birthday?"

Jess turned to the window. Snow was falling heavier now, steady and beautiful. "Tell them..." her voice faltered.

"Jess," Candy said softly, hearing everything anyway.

"I'm glad it's her. Of course, it's her. She is perfect with him. I love them both. I just..."

"You're allowed to feel more than one thing at once."

Jess nodded, even though Candy couldn't see. "He was my person for a long time. But it never would've worked the way we needed it to."

"Nope. But that doesn't mean letting go didn't hurt."

Jess looked down at the scuffed floorboards, already bare in the corners, covered in damp boot prints and specks of salt. "He's going to be a dad."

"He already is," Candy said gently. "You saw it happen the moment he knew she was carrying his kid."

Something inside Jess eased.

"Do me a favor?" she asked, her voice a little brighter. "I need a recipe. Stove-top only. Something warm. I'm cooking for the guests tomorrow, and the oven's out unless Graham gets that generator running. Something simple. Real."

Ooh, cozy-chic breakfast emergency. I got you. It's mostly hashbrowns, cheddar, eggs, and love. Might need a little babysitting, but it was one of my momma's favorites.

"Perfect." Jess laughed, wiping a tear from her cheek. "If I screw this up, I'm blaming the altitude."

I'll send a prayer with the recipe," Candy promised. "Take care of those sweet girls and that grumpy innkeeper—I like where this snowstorm's headed."

When the call ended, Jess slipped her phone into her pocket and stepped onto the enclosed back porch. The sky had turned pale, with the horizon obscured by thick, swirling white clouds. She took a deep breath.

She thought of Jackson holding a newborn. Of Molly, caught between pain and wonder.

And of herself—standing in a borrowed cardigan, supervising cocoa and glitter safety, with heartbeats echoing through every corner of the house.

Chapter Thirteen

Jessica

Clara was the first one to say it.

"I'm bored."

She flopped onto the living room rug and stared at the ceiling with a dramatic sigh worthy of a Hollywood stage.

Noelle, sitting next to her, let out a melodramatic groan. "We've already made cotton ball snowmen, sang carols, and finished two puzzles. One of them was really hard—with, like, a million candy canes."

Jess asked from the loveseat, "How about another game?"

"All the games are boring," Noelle moaned, collapsing like a fainting goat across Clara's legs.

The twins had been stuck inside all morning, and it showed. Outside, snow blanketed the ridge. The bushes, trees, and even the buildings just beyond the porch disappeared under a layer of white.

Inside, the parlor felt like the inside of a snow globe—quiet, still, pretty...and very, very small.

Without power, Jess did what she could. She heated water on the stove, kept the fire going, and unearthed a mountain of board games. But even Clara—who usually loved anything with rules—had given up halfway through Rummikub.

Out of habit, Jess looked toward the kitchen. She had just cleared away the last of breakfast. That's when she remembered something from her earlier chat with Helen: traditions.

"Didn't y'all say there's some special eggnog thing for Christmas Eve?" she asked, pushing off the armrest and standing.

Noelle popped up like a prairie dog. "You mean THE eggnog?"

Clara gasped. "Are we allowed?"

"I'm the grownup on duty," Jess said with a shrug. "Feels like I get to say yes. Plus, we need to use up the fridge stuff anyway."

Squeals—full-bodied, wall-bouncing squeals. The girls hurried down the back hallway before Jess could even ask where the recipe was.

She followed them, tired but amused—and painfully aware she hadn't looked in a mirror all day.

Clara reappeared in the kitchen, holding a flour-dusted recipe box as if it were a museum piece. "Daddy keeps it in his room."

Noelle was already on the stepstool, pulling mixing bowls from the cabinet. "We need the BIG one. That's the one Grandma always used."

Jess laughed. "Team nostalgia, got it."

Clara carefully opened the box, her small hands steady.

Nestled among brittle, curling recipe cards and a paper clip with a faded heart sticker, one card sat, slightly bowed at the edges, its corners softened from handling. She lifted it out and handed it to Jess with both hands.

Jess took it gently. "Is that—?" she asked, then read the title.

Great-Granny Latham's Traditional Holly House Eggnog

The card was thick and textured, made from durable index stock that had survived decades of holidays. It was speckled with faint stains—cinnamon, maybe, or a splash of nutmeg-spiced something from a long-ago Christmas. One corner curled, water-warped and delicate. At the top edge, a faint thumb-shaped smudge darkened the faded blue ink, as if someone had paused there many times, reading the opening words.

Clara began to read over her shoulder. "Six eggs, sugar, whole milk, heavy cream, vanilla, nutmeg, bar-boon"

"Bourbon," Jess corrected. "We can do that part last. There'll be kid and grown-up versions."

"Eggnog's okay," Noelle said thoughtfully. "It smells nice. But I only like a little."

"Same," Clara agreed. "It feels weird on my tongue."

"That's fair. We'll set some aside," Jess grinned. "So, Clara—what's step one?"

"Beat the eggs," Clara said seriously.

"I got it!" Noelle raised her hand, reaching for an egg as if it owed her money.

"No!" Jess caught it just in time. "With a whisk, please. Let me show you."

The kitchen erupted into chaos that would've given Graham a coronary.

Eggshells crunched underfoot. Sugar dusted the counter in uneven piles. Noelle—wild-eyed, with a whisk and nutmeg streaked across her apron and everywhere else—elbowed Clara every time she tried to reread the instructions.

And Jess?

Jess was in the middle of all of it. Standing at the stove, she stirred cream in a saucepan, one hand on the whisk, while the other kept Noelle away from a puddle of yolk with a hip bump.

"Okay," Clara read aloud, "next step: Temper the eggs. Slowly. Don't scramble them.'"

"Yes, chef," Jess said with a salute.

She gauged the cinnamon by instinct. Eyeballed the cream. Halfway through whipping, her arms began to burn. "That's probably good enough, right?"

"More!" Noelle shouted.

"Ugh, fine." Jess groaned, switching arms and rolling up her sleeves. The girls joined in: "Whip it! Whip it!"

By the time the eggnog was thick and glossy, Jess was exhausted—but the thick, creamy liquid looked exactly right. Noelle inhaled deeply and sighed, "Just like Grandma made it."

"You haven't even tried it yet."

Jess poured the eggnog into a vintage cut-glass pitcher from the dining room hutch.

There were traditions in this house. Ones you could feel even if no one said them aloud. Ordinary ingredients took on meaning when prepared in a way that recalled someone else's touch. Laughter in the kitchen felt like a legacy. And old recipes done right eased the pain of loved ones gone.

"I think we did it," Jess said, placing mugs on the table.

Noelle already had hers halfway to her lips. "Can we toast?" she asked. "Just a sip?"

"Absolutely."

Clara raised hers, pinky up. "To us."

Noelle tapped mugs. "And to snow days."

Jess hesitated just a beat. Then, softly: "To remembering what's special about our time together."

The mugs clinked. The eggnog was rich and slightly too thick—just right.

As the girls ran to deliver samples to the guests, Jess leaned against the counter with her arms loosely crossed.

This shouldn't work. This whole thing. She belonged two hundred miles away, in a clinic she'd built from the ground up with grit and caffeine. A place where her name was on the door, her shoes pinched by noon, and the only thing frothy was the foam on her quick-to-go lattes.

Not here. Not in a farmhouse kitchen, waiting for a snowstorm, apron askew, and hair full of nutmeg after a third-grade level eggnog fiasco, and yet, she'd never felt more herself.

She moved around the kitchen on autopilot, stacking dishes and wiping counters one by one. Still, her muscles kept humming with the rhythm of it all. She could still hear Noelle insisting that cinnamon must be sprinkled with flourish, "or it doesn't count," and Clara solemnly double-checking that the eggs were, in fact, 'large' as written. The measuring cups had migrated halfway across the room and were stacked like the Leaning Tower of Sticky. Someone—most likely Noelle—had written "NOG TIME" in cocoa powder across the cutting board.

Jess laughed under her breath as she peeled up the word with a damp cloth.

It shouldn't work.

But the ache in her cheeks showed she had been smiling too long to deny it.

There was something about the kind of mess children made when they weren't rushing—for school, for bedtime, for growing up. This had been deliberate chaos. It was an orchestrated mess. They'd created something out of joy, and it was loud. Gooey.

And still—she would carry it back with her. Not just the thought of eggnog, but the smaller things—the sticky warmth of little hands, the trust of a passed-down tradition that's been remade.

She smiled quietly as she rinsed the rubber spatula, suddenly convinced. This might be the most sacred moment she'd ever felt in a kitchen. There were no sterile prep trays, frozen meals, or stained coffee mugs. Just sweetness, laughter, and centuries-old eggnog that had apparently given the same gift of connection to generations before her.

Outside, the wind rattled the windows. The storm wasn't over. But here, the kitchen still glowed with the ghosts of cookie sprinkles and cheer. She belonged.

And that's when she saw it—the note scribbled in younger handwriting at the bottom of the card.

Use the good mugs. It's never about the eggnog, anyway.

Jess traced a finger over the fading ink.

She was starting to believe that.

The back door swung open with a bang, and a gust of

wind and a loud thud of boots followed. Graham burst into the kitchen, covered in snow and grinning like he'd just hit a jackpot.

"I got it!" he said, breathless.

Jess turned toward him, tea towel over her shoulder. "The generator?"

He nodded, hair and flannel dripping wet. "We'll have the basics up and running soon. Just need to bolt it all back together."

"Nice work," she said, surprised by how alive he looked. Not guarded. Not brooding. Just...himself.

Graham's eyes flicked to the stove. To the pitcher. To the familiar recipe card.

"Did you make...eggnog?"

Jess straightened. "The girls brought me the recipe. I thought—"

His hand hovered over the box, fingertips brushing past the recipe before pulling back. "Where'd they find that?"

"In your room, apparently."

Jess carefully put the card back in the box. "I'm sorry if I overstepped."

He paused for a moment, silent and torn.

Finally, he asked, "Would it be okay if I had a glass?"

Jess exhaled. "Of course."

She ladled the eggnog into one of the good mugs. No chips, with a holly print along the side.

"Do you want the adult version?"

"Adult?"

"Bourbon, rum, or whiskey," she said, already walking to

the pantry shelf. "Pick your poison."

He looked out the window, where another gust of snow hit the porch. "Well, I still have to go back out...but a little rum couldn't hurt. Might even thaw me out a bit."

Jess grinned. She liked that version of him—the dry humor sneaking in beneath the tired lines on his face. She grabbed the rum from the pantry and poured some into his cup before sloshing some into her own.

The first sip caused him to pause.

He blinked, then brought the mug closer to his face as if the smell alone might fill in the gaps that memory couldn't quite reach.

Blinking. "You made this?"

"Yeah," she said. "We followed the recipe. Clara was insistent."

It's...close. Something feels different, but I can't quite put my finger on it.

Jess raised her mug. "Could've been the stove. Or my questionable measuring."

"No," he said, softening. "It's really good."

He didn't move, nor did she.

It tastes exactly the same as when I was a little kid.

There it was. The ache behind the compliment.

Jess sipped her drink, letting the rum burn. Outside, the wind howled against the inn.

"It's getting worse," Jess said.

He nodded. "I should get back out. Dusk's coming."

He set the mug down as if he'd prefer our another drink instead of heading back out into the snow.

Jess tapped the counter with a spoon. "I'll save the rest for you."

"You don't have to—"

"Too late," she said. "There'll be a whole pitcher chilling in the fridge. It should finish cooling quickly once that generator's back up."

He looked at her, and she understood it was about more than just a drink.

She hadn't just followed a recipe. She'd given him something grief had taken—a piece of happiness. A memory. A small comfort amid the storm.

"Go fix the generator," she nodded toward the door. "And, hurry up so you can come back inside and rest."

Chapter Fourteen

Graham

On the back porch, Graham stomped the snow from his boots before reaching for the doorknob, his fingers stiff with cold. The patio thermometer had fallen faster than expected, and ice was frosting over the steps despite the salt he'd sprinkled. The generator was running, powering the fridge, stove, and enough outlets for flashlights, phones, space heaters, and lights on the main level. It wasn't fancy, but it would get them through the next day or two until the county showed up to fix the lines.

The door creaked open, and heat warmed his cheeks as he stepped inside.

"Hey! You made it back just in time," Jess called from around the corner, moments before she appeared with her hair looped into a braided twist, cardigan sleeves rolled to the elbows, apron tied casually at her waist, and dusted with flour. "Coat off. Don't track snow."

Graham blinked.

She'd taken over the kitchen—and brunch—with the kind

of quiet command he imagined served her well at the clinic. The parlor was full. Guests had gathered to stay warm and pass the time, tucked into cozy corners, furniture rearranged around the fireplace. Platters of food lined the coffee bar.

And he...he felt useless.

He slowly hung up his coat, eyes adjusting.

Noelle hurried by with a bowl of rolls. "Dad! Jess let me stir the soup and told me not to touch anything hot! I didn't! Except my tongue. But man, it's good!"

"She let Clara cut vegetables," Noelle added proudly. "And I got to arrange the rolls. After lunch, I get to ring the cocoa bell."

Graham looked down at her. "There's a cocoa bell?"

"You've been gone too long," she teased, twirling away.

The brunch was modest, but lively: a rich vegetable and beef soup, fluffy yeast rolls, and a vibrant salad with both creamy and vinaigrette dressings. Small bowls of toppings like cheese, onions, and croutons were placed between the serving dishes.

In the very center sat a pitcher of eggnog.

It looked exactly like it used to—glossy, gold, and poured into the same footed glass mugs with gold rims that Maggie insisted on every Christmas Eve. He knew Jess had pulled it together, but he also saw how much the girls had been watching—how much they remembered from past years. It wasn't the only time eggnog had appeared since Maggie passed, but it was the first time the girls had made it happen.

"How's the generator?" Jess asked as she appeared beside him.

He looked down. "Good enough. You fixed...everything

else."

A faint flush appeared on her cheeks. "Clara and Noelle were relentless. The guests chipped in. Helen is oddly good at buffet strategy. I just made sure a few things happened."

He didn't say, *you* made sure my things happened, but the words lingered in the space between them.

He nodded toward the pitcher. "Thanks for saving me some."

"I just put it out. You want traditional or the good stuff?"

"Better make it strong," he said, rubbing his shoulder. "That wind's no joke."

"I added a splash of bourbon, this time." She handed him a mug. Their fingers brushed briefly. Too brief.

He gently held it in both hands. The cut glass revealed creamy layers, a fluffy top, and a dusting of nutmeg. It was more than festive—it felt familiar. Heavy with memories.

He took a sip.

Nutmeg. Vanilla. Cream. A little burn as it went down. *Perfect.*

It tasted like that Christmas when Maggie made snowmen out of Sno Balls and sprinkled red, white, and green on the cookies. Jess had changed something—richer—but the core was the same.

Across the room, she was laughing as Noelle launched into a wildly uncoordinated version of the Nutcracker for a trio of delighted guests. Jess refilled napkin baskets and smiled through it all.

The mug hovered at his lips longer than it should have.

The first sip was warm, sweet, and sharp with nostalgia. Jess had poured it exactly right—light on the bourbon, heavy on the memory. A flicker of cinnamon. A hum of vanilla. The kind of drink that goes down too smoothly when a man's guard is down.

He took another one. And then another.

Each swallow eased something shaky in his chest, spreading warmth from the inside out, like a spring thaw slowly seeping through frost-bitten ground.

His gaze shifted to Jess as she bent down to pick up a stray napkin, her hair loosening from a twist, curls brushing the soft pink of her cheek. She was laughing at something Noelle had said.

He gripped the mug tighter.

It wasn't indulgence, he told himself.

He'd earned this. The generator was humming again, the propane was holding, no one was cold or hungry, and the girls were happy enough to spill marshmallows across the parlor and call it decorating.

So, what if he took a moment?

One sip for surviving. Another for keeping everything upright. A third for finally—just for once—not having to do it all alone.

It wasn't about the bourbon, grief, or the hollow ache he mostly ignored this time of year. It was about acknowledging survival, quietly filling an empty space in a way that felt natural to him. No speeches or thank-yous. Just a deep breath, a mug in his hand, and the rare comfort of stillness without fear.

The mug found his lips again. He didn't mean to finish it.

But he had.

And when he reached for the pitcher again, the tip of the bourbon bottle softly clinked against the rim, and the truth stirred quietly in his chest.

Maybe it wasn't only nostalgia.

Maybe it was the ache of something returning.

Focusing on feeling rather than managing.

Of hoping instead of holding everything back.

Graham poured another.

By the time Helen nudged him with a knit coaster and a wink, he was warm enough to sink into a parlor wingback with a long, deep exhale.

"I did a good job picking your second in command," she whispered.

He didn't argue.

Music played softly from Jess's Bluetooth speaker, tucked behind the cocoa pitcher. Not jingly or bright—something string-heavy and nostalgic, like crackling records and handwritten letters. It filled the corners without crowding them, the way lamplight softened the old wood.

The girls floated through the room like tiny parade queens, handing out napkins with curtsies and official titles—"Lady Helen," "Sir Malcolm," "Most Esteemed Snowman Builder." Each piece of fabric was creased and crooked, with some smudged with glitter and others tied with ribbon. A jumble of charm and childhood precision.

No one seemed to mind. They adored it.

The honeymooners snuggled close, appearing flushed and happy. Helen and her husband sat by the window, cups gently clinking, smiling over whispered jokes.

And Jess—

She moved through the heart of everything, sleeves rumpled, apron askew, cheeks flushed from laughter. A holly-shaped barrette clung to her hair—probably a leftover from Noelle's crafts. Her smile—when it reached Graham—was quiet and bright.

Something twisted inside him.

Not grief. Not duty. Something softer. Yet more dangerous. A flutter in the ribs whispering: *You're not alone anymore.*

He shifted in his seat, trying to ignore it. But it didn't fade.

In a relentless effort to keep the girls busy, Jess found the supplies to roast marshmallows near the fire. It didn't take long before they were covered in chocolate and graham cracker crumbs. The air smelled of roasted sugar and pine. Joy buzzed through the room—not polished, but genuine. Built from mismatched dishes and makeshift plans.

And Jess?

Jess moved in the middle of it as if she'd always been there. Not taking up space but making it. Creating a home.

Graham felt it settle in his chest: how family can be a gift—and how risky it is to want someone to keep creating it. To want to keep experiencing it with her.

By the time brunch wound down—crumbs cleared, laughter echoing upstairs—he stood up.

And the room tilted.

Not much. Just enough.

He swayed.

Jess caught his eye. "You, okay?"

"Just...need to sit for a minute."

Or get some air. Or reset. He muttered something about the generator and ducked out. Jess watched him go, brow furrowed slightly, but didn't follow.

She gave him space.

Which was good, because he only made it to the back stairwell before sitting down, bracing his head in one hand, trying not to look as green as he felt.

Damn eggnog.

He pressed his knuckles to his temple and counted backward from twenty.

Footsteps approached.

He prepared his excuses, but Jess didn't say anything. She just sat next to him, their knees touching. She held out a cool cloth and a bottle of water.

He accepted both and pressed the cloth to the back of his neck. Exhaled slowly.

"Old family recipe," she murmured. "Should've come with a warning label."

He didn't laugh, but damn if he wasn't grateful.

So he sipped the water, closed his eyes, and let her sit beside him in silence...until the spinning stopped.

"I didn't eat much," he admitted, swallowing against the sharp flicker building behind his ribs. "Probably the eggnog."

"The girls barely touched theirs," she said, sliding her arm under his.

He let out a breathy laugh. "Or I finally hit a wall."

"We all hit walls," she murmured.

"Can I ask you a question?" Graham slurred slowly.

Jess watched him, partly to make sure he hadn't poisoned

himself and partly to gauge what his question might be. "Sure, but make it an easy one."

"Do you want a family?"

"Damn, just throwing out the heavy hitters, huh?"

Graham looked at her, panic in his eyes. He patted her knee. "I'm sorry, I didn't mean it like that." He waved his hand around. "It's just that you're here alone...and you're beautiful." He looked her in the eyes, and for a moment, his gaze was dead sober. "I can't understand it."

Jess thought about giving him a sarcastic reply to his obvious lack of manners, but she also knew it was probably the eggnog talking. "I had a chance at a family once, but it wasn't right for me. I'm no longer close to my family. We drifted apart for different reasons. But, even when we were together, it wasn't all that great. There was a lot of fighting...and drinking. Honestly, when I had the chance to create a home of my own, I could never have imagined it looking like this...like the home you've built at the Holly House." She reached over and placed her hand on his knee. "I can see what a real home and family look like now."

"I'm sorry—"

"Don't be." She braced her hand on her knee and began to stand. "If you really want to know, yes, I want a family." What she didn't say was: *Yes, I'd like a family just like this one.*

Instead, she helped him up, matching his slow steps through the hallway. Her shoulder pressed calmly against his side.

In the family suite, the lights were dim, and the battery-operated lamp cast everything in a warm, golden glow. The bed had been turned down, extra pillows fluffed, and the quilt smoothed.

"You planned this?" he asked, blinking.

"Clara said you hadn't slept. Even soldiers need rest, Walker."

At the foot of the bed, he rubbed his temple. "Could be food poisoning."

"Maybe. The recipe uses raw eggs." She placed a water glass on the nightstand.

"That's what was different," he mumbled, groaning. "Margaret switched to pasteurized years ago."

"Could also be bourbon on an empty stomach, and/or exhaustion."

"Don't accuse me of being soft."

"Never," she said. "Just tired."

She lifted the covers. "Boots off."

He grumbled but sat down. Jess crouched and gently unlaced them. He blinked at her closeness.

"You're really tucking me in?"

"Want me to call one of the girls?"

"Point made."

He eased back into the bed with a groan. Jess tucked the quilt to his chest, then added another pillow.

"Stay elevated," she said. "Also...barf bowl."

She placed it near the baseboard. Far enough to preserve his dignity, but close enough to grab in an emergency.

Graham cracked an eye. "You're dangerous, Doc."

"I'm practical," she replied. "Dangerous comes later."

He smiled—barely—and let his head fall into the pillow.

She dimmed the lamp on her way out, casting the room in honeyed hush, softening the worn corners of the wood, the old knitting basket by the rocker, and the heap of folded laundry he'd probably meant to put away.

Graham didn't see her go.

He was already asleep.

Chapter Fifteen

Jessica

The first time she checked on Graham, he was still asleep.

Jess paused in the doorway for a breath or two, just long enough to confirm the rise and fall of the quilt meant everything was okay. The scent of cedar and laundry filled the room. His coat still hung over the rocker; boots tucked neatly beside it. One arm had worked free from the blanket, fingers splayed across the coverlet like he was bracing for something, even in sleep.

She set a fresh glass of water on the nightstand, adjusted the blanket to cover his shoulder, and winced when a floorboard creaked under her heel. He didn't stir.

Downstairs, the hush had finally settled in.

Dinner had been simple—spaghetti with meat sauce and the last of the lunch rolls. Everyone had pitched in to keep their hands busy after a long, quiet day. Helen and her husband turned in around seven. The honeymooners returned a borrowed deck of cards and disappeared soon after. The extra marshmallows had been tucked into a bowl with plastic wrap for tomorrow's cocoa. Jess had gone through the parlor twice, just to make sure no books, mugs, or rumpled blankets had been forgotten.

The glow remained—soft lights, soft gratitude—but it had softened now, settling around the beams instead of blazing from the fire. She lit the candle on the kitchen windowsill, the last task before calling it a night.

Or so she thought.

The twins found her near the beverage bar, locked in a solemn debate over dried mini marshmallows (float better) versus fresh (melt better). Noelle had glitter dusted behind one ear from a paper chain accident. Clara looked ready to argue the benefits of marshmallow foam over sprinkles.

"We have something else we need to do," Clara declared, arms crossed.

Jess shrugged and said, "Something besides drinking three cups of cocoa and launching into a sugar coma?"

"It's Christmas Eve," Noelle whispered, eyes wide. "And we forgot the most important part."

Jess looked around, trying to figure out what they'd missed. "Salt on the steps? Cocoa rations? Battery check?"

"The tree," Clara whispered. "Our tree."

Noelle nodded solemnly. "We always had one in the family room. Not big. Just ours."

Jess blinked, her chest tugging gently. "The parlor tree's not enough?"

"It's for everyone," Clara explained. "But it's not the same. Mama had one for the family in the suite. With special ornaments. Grandma keeps them in the closet now."

"In Dad's closet," Noelle added sweetly. "But don't worry. We can get them."

Jess hesitated—then nodded. "Okay. Let's do it."

Clara and Noelle sprinted off, chattering about supplies and whether ornaments or candy canes were the superior tree decoration. Jess lingered for a moment, resting one palm against the hallway wall to steady herself. This had to be the right call.

She glanced back toward the primary bedroom where Graham finally slept. He'd carried too much for too long, and this morning...

This morning had cracked something open in her.

She hadn't meant to overstep with the eggnog. She'd only wanted to offer something warm, something joyful. A thread of memory for the girls. But Graham's reaction had reminded her—kindness, given carelessly, could cut too.

That recipe wasn't just nostalgia. It was grief. It was his wife's handwriting in the margins.

She respected that now. Respected him.

But this moment with the girls? This was different.

The girls had always had this to hold on to. She knew how hard Graham had worked this year to preserve all the holiday traditions, and how he'd had to let things go. She didn't want this to be another moment, remembered later as a holiday tradition lost because that was 'the year the storm came.'

And Graham? He deserved rest. He deserved to miss a tradition and not carry the guilt of it.

She drew in a breath and straightened. This wasn't about fixing things. It was about making space—for him to heal, for them to hold joy. This wasn't overstepping. It was an offering. Quiet. Intentional.

She rolled up her sleeves and headed to the kitchen, passing under the garland they'd made the day before. Somewhere behind her, Noelle shouted something about sparkles being 'tree-mendous,' and Clara groaned.

Let this be something they remember for the warmth, not the weight.

The porch tree wasn't much—maybe four feet tall, more twig than fir—but the girls carried it between them with enthusiasm. In the sitting room, Jess rolled up the rug and rearranged two wingbacks to make space in a cozy corner. She tucked a pair of battery tea lights beneath the branches to give the little tree its glow.

Clara slipped quietly into her dad's bedroom and returned with a single box.

"There," she whispered, her face reverent.

A single box, clearly labeled in thin, looping pen: *Margaret's Christmas.* Years of corner wear and the faded red bow told a richer story than the Sharpie ever could.

Jess crouched beside them. "Are you sure?" she asked gently.

Noelle nodded. "Mom would want it to be pretty."

They made sure the bedroom door behind them was closed and settled into the sitting room parlor before lifting the lid.

Inside the box lay a folded paper angel. Bits of burlap and velvet, cinnamon sticks bundled with twine. Tiny beads were hot-glued onto pine cones. Margaret's name was painted in shaky preschool block letters across a clothespin Santa head. Next to it were two more Santas with the girls' names written on the backs. Jess didn't need a DNA test to know which ones Margaret's hands had helped shape.

They worked in a hush, careful and unhurried.

Jess let them lead.

The ornaments jingled softly, as memories settled back into place. Jess tied a red thread around a set of three twine stars. Clara adjusted a crooked felt penguin until it stood tall. Noelle topped it with a shimmering silver bow scavenged from a peppermint tin.

"This one always went in the middle," Noelle said, draping a beaded loop. "From the year Daddy burned the pie."

Jess smiled. "Sounds legendary."

"He tried a hand mixer in the pumpkin mix," Clara said flatly.

"It exploded," Noelle added. "Even got in the stove."

They looked pleased about it now.

They added paper chains made from old design catalogs—at least two pages of holiday toy lists now permanently glitter-glued into garland.

When the tree was finished, they gathered on the rug.

Jess fetched the Santa plate and filled it with two cookies, plus a note in highlighter ink: *Dear Santa, long night? Have a snack.* She added half a cocoa and a sprig of holly from outside.

"No carrots?" she teased.

Clara rolled her eyes. "The reindeer get snacks in the barn. That's where the real food is."

"Obviously," Jess said, grinning.

Then the room was still. Not with silence exactly, but with something soft and full.

The girls leaned in. Noelle's head settled on Jess's shoulder. Clara pressed close on the other side.

They didn't ask for a story. Didn't need one. Jess wrapped a throw around all three of them and held on.

It was Clara who broke the quiet.

"Thanks," she whispered.

"For what?"

"For helping Daddy," Noelle murmured. "And us."

Clara nodded. "For helping us remember."

Jess pulled them tighter. "Thanks for letting me."

Clara looked up, serious. "You make the house feel big again."

Jess blinked hard.

Then tucked them both into her arms.

By the time their eyes began to flutter shut, Jess had slid a hand across each little shoulder, slow and sure, anchoring them in comfort. She guided them onto their beds and tucked the blankets up to their chins.

Careful as a wish whispered over cocoa, she dimmed the lights and padded across the room.

She paused at the dresser.

Their handmade snow globes stood in a row, each imperfect in its own way. Clara's held a lopsided snowman and a lone pine tree, Noelle's a reindeer leaping through gold glitter, and Jess's had a small red gift box and two bottle-brush trees tipped just off center, swirling with a sparkle that never quite settled.

She picked it up. The jar was cool in her hands.

She gave it a shake.

The glitter rose and spun—suspended like a breath held

too long—before falling in slow, shimmering spirals. The trees swayed inside, and Jess whispered a wish.

Let this be a Christmas they remember for the laughter, not the loss.

She set the globe gently beside the others.

Something inside her was settling now. Not because everything was perfect—but because something imperfect could hold space, too.

In this inn, at this moment, in this soft, glitter-covered house full of people who didn't need her polished—they needed her present.

And maybe that's why she made the wish.

Not for the storm to pass.

But for something inside her to stay.

She turned, pulled the blanket tighter around her shoulders, and slipped back into the soft-lit hallway.

Chapter Sixteen

Jessica

Every room in the inn had gone quiet, wrapped in the soft silence of deep snow and the memory of tired laughter. The fire in the parlor had sputtered out to embers hours ago. Now, everything was soft. Still.

Jess lay on the narrow couch in the Walker family suite, cocooned in a thick plaid blanket, eyes wide open against the darkness. There was still too much of the day left bouncing around her mind for her to sleep.

Through the door on the other side of the room, Clara and Noelle breathed in tandem, tucked under quilts in their twin beds. The little tree they'd decorated glowed faintly, its battery-powered base flickering every few seconds, tossing slivers of gold across the ceiling. One ornament—a crooked candy cane covered in sequins—spun slowly on a fishing line, catching stray shadows and light.

Jess sat up, careful not to wake the girls.

She slipped out of the warmth of the blanket and padded

across the wooden floor barefoot to the sitting-room window. Jess curled into the corner of the built-in bench seat, one knee propped, a second blanket making a messy nest pile for her head.

Outside, the snow lay soft and heavy across the porch roof, windowsills, and trees beyond. Even now, it was still falling—barely. Just a whisper of flakes twirling against a charcoal sky. Snow clung to everything in delicate waves, smoothing the angles of the world. No edges, no traffic, no hurry.

Under the eaves, the pine branches drooped, faintly silver in the moonlight. A string of Christmas lights one floor above glowed steadily against the snowbank. The porch garland, now frozen, shimmered faintly with frost—sleepy and glittering and utterly still.

But above?

The sky was velvet.

Deep and enormous, and filled with stars. Dozens, then hundreds. Some twinkled clean-white. Others blushed gold, soft-pink, a single icy blue. She couldn't remember the last time she'd seen stars like this. She couldn't remember the last time she had let herself slow down long enough to notice which way Orion tilted, or how wide the sky stretched when there weren't high-rises in the way.

In Serenity, the lights of her clinic had been constant. She never left work at a decent hour. Her on-call bag sat at the foot of her stairs almost year-round. There were patient files bookmarked on her laptop, voicemail pings she never cleared. She'd built something good—necessary.

But sitting here...

That life felt two dimensions flatter than this snow-chalked wonderland, this quiet inn full of warmth and soft chaos.

She let her forehead rest against the window. It was cold, and that grounded her.

White frost bloomed along the outer edge of the pane, curling like lace near her temple. Beneath it, the gardens slept. The trail past the porch edge had vanished beneath drifts, and gone completely were the footprints of the day.

The branches drooped, and the world held still, but everything inside her felt like it was shifting.

How long had it been since she'd been still? Not paused. Not waiting. But truly still—no purpose, no list.

When had she stopped noticing that her body only relaxed when it was forced to? That she hadn't built rest into her life at all?

Noelle had said something earlier—head full of glitter and marshmallows and big, certain declarations.

"This house makes wishes grow."

And despite trying to hold on to healthy amounts of skepticism, Jess was starting to believe her. She pulled the blanket tighter, tucking her knees to her chest. Her toes brushed the soft fibers of the thick rug.

She smiled faintly and leaned her head back, staring out again at the stillness sprawling across the ridge and the town that lay hibernating beneath it all, tucked in under layers of snow and shimmer and memory.

The walk back to her real life would wait. Her emails would wait.

For now...*this.*

Right here.

This family, this inn, this impossible, joyful week had cracked something open she wasn't sure she could close again.

Her thoughts softened. Her heart didn't ache—it settled.

She hadn't expected roots to grow in the snow.

But maybe it wasn't about expectations.

Maybe some homes don't require planning.

Some just welcome you in and keep you warm until you're ready to stay.

And she was coming to understand she didn't need to wait for the storm to pass to realize she'd already found something worth coming back for.

As the stars burned bright above the ridge, Jess slipped sideways into the blanket, curled back into the window seat, and closed her eyes.

She fell asleep as golden glitter danced through her dreams, confident that her wish had already been granted.

Chapter Seventeen

Graham

The first thing Graham noticed was the quiet. Like a time traveler, the lure of sleep had transported him into the future. He'd drifted off to the sounds of laughing guests, playful kids, and holiday cheer. Now, the house was enveloped in silence.

He was familiar with Holly House's usual night hush. It was never completely quiet, with the furnace humming beneath the floor and condensation dripping from the gutters on the porch roof. But this was something more profound—still yet warm. Holly House felt like it was on pause. Comfort settled low in his ribs instead of the usual worry and the ache of grief. No one needed him, and everything felt alright.

He inhaled carefully. No nausea. No fuzz behind his vision. The worst had passed.

The bedroom was dim, lit only by the warm flicker of the battery-powered lantern near the window, casting long shadows along the pine-paneled walls. His body felt sluggish but stable as he tested the pull of gravity and swung his legs off the mattress.

One step. Then another. No dizziness. His breath remained steady.

He tugged at the thermal shirt he'd worn to bed—it was wrinkled and clung to one side. His hair, already tousled before, had gone full rooster-tail at the back. Whatever. He could fix it later. Right now, something in the air had shifted.

Graham crossed the room slowly and pressed his hand to the doorframe, every movement involuntarily careful, as if he expected his body to revolt at any moment. He pushed the door open.

The family sitting room had transformed.

In the far corner, tucked between the reading lamp and the quilt basket, stood a four-foot-tall pine tree. It was barely large enough to fill the space, yet it radiated in a way that slowly sucker-punched him. Its branches reached out wide, pieced together in personality rather than symmetry. Warm red ribbons looped among sprigs of holly, and sparkling gold stars shimmered from their strings, crooked but proud. Ornaments crowded the center. Some were glass, some paper, and one suspiciously looked like it was made from an old clothespin and too much glitter.

At the base, a faded satin tree skirt pooled gently, with the corners folded under in soft waves. It looked like something Margaret might have hemmed years ago, with uneven stitching—crooked but made by hand rather than rushed. One corner featured a tiny, stitched M.

Jess must have found *the box*. He stepped forward, drifting closer, pulled by something quieter than curiosity.

A paper chain stretched across the far window, each link a different color and size, no two quite matching. Most of them were folded, twisted, or slightly ink-stained. There were finger-prints on a few, sparkles where there probably shouldn't be, smudges where crayons had pressed too hard. Graham's throat tightened at the sight. His girls had made those.

On the tree, a chipped wooden reindeer tilted sideways near the top. Below it hung the snowman Margaret always tucked near the trunk, half-hidden, like a secret joke only he and Eleanor ever understood. Seeing it again now—witnessing how the girls had placed it, not tucked away but right out front—nearly undid him.

He hadn't heard a thing. They must've done it while he slept.

Slowly, he moved farther into the room, feet bare against the scuffed wood. Something tugged inside him with every step—he didn't know if it was awe, guilt, or gratitude. Maybe all three.

On the coffee table sat a tray: two cookies on a Santa-themed plate, a bundle of holly tied with baker's twine, and a note in Noelle's handwriting.

FOR SANTA. Merry CHRISTMAS!!! P.S. Don't eat too many. Dad says sugar is bad for you. Noelle and Clara

He huffed a laugh. Of course.

He turned toward the couch—and stopped.

Jess was there, curled under a patchwork throw, dozing in the corner of the window seat. The flickering glow from the small battery lights under the tree bathed her in soft gold, catching the tips of her loose braid. She looked like she belonged there...and not just tonight.

He reached for the back of the armchair and steadied himself before he folded to sit beside her quietly, careful not to wake her, but selfish enough to want to be near her.

He looked back at the tree. This wasn't an invasion. This was caregiving. There was no carefully orchestrated plan to 'fix Christmas' and she certainly wasn't trying to replace old traditions or old memories.

Instead, Jess bridged the gap. She helped the girls take the pieces of memory and make them their own.

The ache that followed wasn't sharp. Just deep.

He rubbed a hand over the back of his neck. If he stayed here too long, that ache would turn into something else. Something bigger. He couldn't let that happen. Not yet.

He stepped away from the tree and pulled a flannel over-shirt from the hook by the door.

The floorboards creaked beneath his weight as he walked down the narrow hallway toward the old basement stairs.

The workshop had always been a place of comfort and reflection for him. It hadn't changed in years.

The same oil-stained pegboard hung on the wall, lined with wrenches and pliers like sentries at their posts. There was the same bench cut from salvaged oak, its grain still splintered at the corners. Along the wall, half-used bolts sat tucked in mayonnaise jars labeled with masking tape, the Sharpie faded but still legible. A patched leather stool waited near the back—its legs uneven, one bolt perpetually too loose.

Graham stepped inside, letting the heavy door creak shut

behind him.

He ran his hand across the top of the workbench, fingers grazing the always-there clutter: a tape measure curled into itself, a half-dead pencil, a mug stained with long-gone coffee, the lip etched from years of use.

He didn't turn on the overhead light. Instead, he reached for the portable lantern looped onto the corner hook and clicked it on. Golden light spread across the scarred wood—wide, soft, imperfect. Familiar.

The top drawer slid open with a soft scrape of wood-on-wood. His old punch set lay inside, nestled in a velvet-lined tin he hadn't touched in too long. Brass-letter stamps, worn clean from years of use.

Next to it was a small box of copper discs, about the size of a biscuit—kept long after he stopped making them for guests. Wedding favors, birth announcements, housewarming tokens. At one point, he even thought about starting a side business, turning metal into keepsakes, but then life changed dramatically.

He thumbed through the pile and picked one near the bottom. It was already smoothed on the edges. The copper felt warm to the touch. His thumb brushed over it and encountered the faintest indentations from where someone, probably himself, had started something and then left it. He didn't remember what it was supposed to become.

But maybe this was better.

He sat on the stool. It wobbled beneath him, a familiar sign of age, uneven from years of use. He didn't bother fixing it. He simply planted his boots firmly on the concrete and settled into its sway, tilting forward until his elbows rested on the bench, and let his shoulders roll into a comfortable curve out of habit.

The copper disc rested against his palm, cool and smooth at first, but quickly absorbing the heat of his skin. There was comfort in the feeling. Anchor. Something solid that could be molded, shaped, and made real.

With a slow breath, he reached for the steel stamps. One by one, he slid them out of the lined tin, the worn edges softly clinking against each other.

His hands felt shaky at first.

Stiff from the cold, from days of chopping wood, wrangling girls, and handling too many small disasters. His fingers weren't used to this kind of delicate work anymore—requiring gentle pressure instead of brute strength.

But the rhythm returned quickly.

Muscle memory long buried was stirred back to life, aided by the sigh of the propane heater in the corner, the clean tin tang of the punch set, and the faint warmth of Jess still lingering under his ribcage.

He placed the copper disc on the flat of the anvil, adjusted it until the surface was smooth and level. His calloused fingers grasped the first stamp, aligning it by instinct rather than plan, and he reached for the ball-peen hammer on the left. Slightly off-balance, but with a cold, familiar weight.

"H," he murmured under his breath. Guiding. Grounding. He lined the letter up, exhaled once, and brought the hammer down with a sharp, controlled tap.

The sound rang out across the workshop, high and crisp, metal singing against metal.

He paused.

Rolled his shoulders once.

Shifted his grip, then reached for the next stamp.

"O." Another strike. Slightly off-center. It echoed shorter—emptier. Not quite right.

Not perfect.

But that didn't bother him anymore.

Perfection wasn't the point. Jess didn't need things curated. She needed the kind of truth you could run your fingers across. Something a little off balance, but still dependable and solid.

His grip grew steadier with each letter. The weight behind the hammer grew easier to time. The rhythm of the strikes came faster, more definitively, as he moved from letter to letter, rotating stamps in and out in a practiced sequence.

"Holly House," he stamped.

A little crooked. Left-leaning. The final curve of the e tucked too close to the edge, but it held.

He held the disc with two fingers and ran his thumb over each newly carved groove. Tiny ridges pressed against his skin, telling an unspoken story engraved letter by letter, each one like the notch of an old tree marking where something meaningful had passed.

He tilted it under the lamp. Light caught in the indentation like water on pavement. The copper glowed orange and gold and was full of quiet memory.

Then, carefully, he laid it flat again and retrieved the holly leaf stamp, found his spot just beneath the second word, and pressed the metal down.

The strike was firm but not too hard, with the hammer

landing a muted knock that rippled through the disc and up his knuckles. There, a swirl of stem with veined edges—a decorative accent Margaret loved but he hadn't used in years. It landed slightly off-center, almost brushing the E

Still, it looked beautiful.

He grabbed a worn-out rag from his back pocket and wiped the surface, removing the raised burrs and metal dust. The copper gently warmed in his hand as he cleaned it, a soft heat spreading from friction and purpose. It almost pulsed.

Turning it over, the unmarked side felt too empty.

Too blank.

This wasn't just a keepsake. This was a conversation in his language—one of gesture, weight, and soul.

Jess wouldn't care if the letters didn't line up right.

She'd never ask for straight edges.

She'd ask what mattered.

And what mattered shone in her smile when she handed out cocoa, in the way she tucked blankets around children that weren't hers, as if it were second nature. It lived in how she made the house feel like it still hummed with hope, with life.

She had undone the silence in him more thoroughly than any hope or holiday ever had.

His jaw clenched.

He reached for the smaller lettering set. Slid one piece out at a time, arranging them gently, whisper-silent against the bench.

And then, slowly and carefully, he stamped:

May you find a life filled with the same joy you've given us.

The letters took longer, the spacing was tighter, and the words curved up toward the disk's edge by the time he hit 'us'.

But it still fit. Every letter mattered, and he hit each one with enough honesty to send them deep into metal and meaning alike.

He paused, studied the line once more, then added, quieter than the rest:

—G

He threaded a red ribbon through the top hole. It was a piece from the craft bin Noelle had dumped across the dining room three days ago, and just the kind of thing Jess would love. Full of joy. Not perfect, but close enough.

Graham didn't hold it long.

Closing the workshop behind him, he moved through the quiet inn. The floorboards barely creaked under his socks, like the house was a conspirator in on the surprise.

On the main floor, the air was warm from the stove and still carried the scent of spice and sugar. The handmade ornaments on the girls' tree cast gentle shadows onto stacked gift boxes and the wrinkled blankets tossed in a heap on the rug. The paper chain shimmered faintly in the dark.

Graham crouched in front of the tree and gently brushed aside a handmade gingerbread ornament Clara had hung crooked earlier in the day. Tucked between two cotton-ball snowdrifts and a strand of pearl garland, he slipped the new ornament onto a lower branch.

The tree twinkled. The copper ornament rested halfway down, amongst the branches, and the other ornaments from all the other people who had made the inn and his family special.

Jess stirred.

He turned as she shifted on the window seat. Her eyes fluttered open, unfocused for a moment before finding his.

"You're up," she said, voice sleep-thick and full of relief.

He nodded. "And you built Christmas while I was knocked out."

She smiled, slow and shy. "The girls asked."

"I guessed as much."

He glanced at the tree again. "How'd you know where the boxes were?"

"The girls knew exactly where to find them."

"Of course they did."

A pause. Not silence exactly, but reverent quiet. Like the room had agreed not to rush them.

"I didn't want you to miss it," she said. "But they…they needed to do this. Not just for her. For themselves."

He nodded once, the reality of it settling in. "You did the right thing."

"You don't mind?"

He looked at her.

Then back at the glowing little tree, standing proud in the corner with its crooked ornaments and glimmering garland made of love and glitter glue.

"No," he said after a long breath. "I think I love it."

Chapter Eighteen

Jessica

Jess was still half-submerged in sleep, the quilt wrapped close around her, when a squeal cracked the quiet.

Then another.

Tiny feet hitting the hardwood.

She blinked just as a fast-moving pajama blur pounced onto the bed.

"It's Christmas!" Noelle cried, arms flung wide.

"You're missing it!" Clara shouted from the doorway, her braid slipping sideways.

Jess blinked again. "I'm—what now?"

She sat upright slowly, blankets slipping from her shoulders, her hand bracing against the warm quilt that definitely hadn't been on the window seat where she'd fallen asleep.

The Juniper Room. Her room.

Not the bench. Not the family suite. Her room's familiar wreath still hung on the inside of the door, and her boots sat untouched by the corner trunk. The lamp on her nightstand flickered faintly, battery-powered but dimming fast.

"I'm in bed," she whispered, blinking hard like that might make the room shift again.

But no, she hadn't imagined it. The bedding was tucked neatly around her torso, as if someone had carefully placed her here. Someone with large, capable hands and a protective streak roughly the size of Holly Ridge.

Her brow furrowed.

The last thing she remembered clearly was waking in the Walker family suite.Graham had been there.

She remembered the light brush of his voice. The way he'd said, *you built Christmas while I was knocked out.*

After that...

The edges blurred, hazy as fog drifting over snow. Except—a fragment surfaced.

Graham's arms, steady beneath her as he lifted her from the window seat, made her feel like she was something fragile....*pr ecious*.

Her cheek had found his shoulder—solid, quiet, warm. She meant to speak, to tell him she could walk, but sleep pulled her in too greedily. Every step had swayed softly, never jostled. She remembered the feel of his fingers curling more securely beneath her knees.

The slow hush of his breath as he carried her down the corridor.

And then *this*. Her room. Her bed. He'd carried her here.

She let out a breathless sort of laugh. Of course, he had.

"He just couldn't let me be the one caring for people," she said to herself.

"Come on," Noelle urged, crawling toward her pillow. "You gotta see it. It's beautiful. Daddy says the snow made the whole yard sparkle."

Jess kicked her legs over the edge, and the quilt slipped off her lap. "Is there cocoa?"

"There will be," Clara promised, already rifling through a basket for socks.

"And lights everywhere," Noelle added. "Daddy fixed everything. He even got the record player plugged into the generator to play the Christmas records!"

Jess rubbed her forehead and smiled. "Are there presents? Maybe...a quiet one?"

Two sets of eyes blinked at her. Clara grinned. "There's one that's just for you."

Noelle's whisper dropped to a conspiratorial pitch. "Daddy hid it. But we found it."

"No, we didn't," Clara huffed. "We waited 'til he told us where to put it. That's not the same."

Jess laughed. "Okay, okay. Lead the way before the tree gets empty."

"Noelle already got two candy canes!" Clara tattled, grabbing Jess's robe from the armchair. "And she licked one!"

"Because it was broken and I was saving it."

Jess pulled her arms through the sleeves and followed them barefoot into the family suite, their laughter trailing ahead.

She stopped at the door.

The tree looked brighter in the morning light, even without electricity—like the silver stars and red-stitched ornaments glowed with their own holiday spirit. Small, wrapped parcels lined the base. They were irregular shapes, decorated with colorful ribbons and tags scribbled in eager handwriting. A few mugs were already filled with marshmallows, and there were cocoa packets nearby. A plate of cookies had been abandoned mid-munch for more exciting discoveries.

And at the center of the tree, nestled between a button-covered snowflake and a crooked felt Santa, hung a copper circle that reflected the twinkle of light from the nearby window—blinking gold one moment, rose-hued the next.

Its edges were slightly uneven, the holly leaf imperfectly pressed into the metal, like the punch had shifted at the last second. Not mass-produced. Hand-etched. Crafted with care and practiced hands.

Jess stepped closer. Her breath caught.

HOLLY HOUSE.

She turned it over with reverence. On the back, a message was pressed in slightly uneven, and imperfect letters:

May you find a life filled with the same joy you've given us.—G

She brushed her thumb across the words. The metal was cool beneath her skin, but something warm bloomed in her.

Behind her, the floor creaked.

Graham stood just a step behind, sock-footed and quietly steady. The pine-green Henley fit snugly over the broad curves of his shoulders, sleeves pushed up to his elbows as if he'd gotten halfway to relaxed and then paused there. His jeans showed gentle signs of wear, slightly frayed at the knees. His hair was still damp from sleep or snow—raked back, with curls gathering at the nape.

"You found it," he said. And she thought maybe he meant more than the ornament.

Jess turned toward him, the O ornament cupped in her palms. "It's beautiful."

A flicker passed over his face—relief, maybe. Or something tender and unsure.

"I made them years ago," he said. "When Margaret was still here. We would pass one out every year—Thanksgiving through New Year's. Guests got to take a piece of the holiday home."

She turned the disc again, watching the way the light danced over the words.

"Margaret always said small things like that..." He hesitated. "That they gave us something to hold onto. Something that made living life solid."

Jess nodded once, her throat thick. "It feels very special."

Graham stepped closer. His hand brushed the back of a chair, as if he wasn't sure where to go, only that he needed to stand beside her.

"I wanted you to know," he said. "How much you've helped, I mean."

Her breath hitched.

He didn't touch her. Didn't reach for her hand. But the space between them pulsed with something electric.

"I couldn't have done it without you," he added. "Not with the same outcome. You've brought joy back into our home...something I didn't even realize was missing. That bone deep, glitter bomb, swirling ribbon, jazz hand joy."

Jess blinked slowly, her chest aching.

She'd spent so many holidays making space for everyone

else.

As if her own wants were indulgent.

As if her desires had expiration dates.

But this—this was a reminder that she could have made joy, too.

She looked down again. Her thumb skimmed the word *us*, the edge catching lightly on a callus she hadn't noticed forming.

"I don't know what joy looks like when I'm not here," she whispered.

Graham smiled—quiet, patient, devastatingly kind. "You'll figure it out."

Jess's eyes shimmered, but she didn't cry.

And softly, just for him: "Thank you."

He nodded—once, deeply. A response that meant:

Any time.

Every time.

The lights on the tree flickered beside them—dim, warm, and perfect.

His hand dropped to the back of the chair. Not to pull. Not to press. Just a promise that he'd still be there when she was ready.

Jess handed the ornament back without a word. He stepped forward and hung it—just beneath the crooked reindeer Clara had placed the night before. Not center stage, but not hidden, either. It belonged there.

Then, padded feet thundered from the hallway.

"Merry Christmas!" Noelle yelled, her red fleece robe flaring behind like a cape. Clara followed, regal and breathless, a paper crown askew on her head.

"You forgot the song!" Clara accused.

"I didn't forget! I started early!"

"Jingle bells," Clara began in a serious alto, "our way, not your way."

"No, no, no," Noelle wailed. "We agreed on *We Wish You a Merry Christmas!* That's the one from our record!"

Jess laughed. The girls spun with excitement in their pajamas—one navy with stars, the other red with gingerbread men.

Graham smiled as one darted past him. "We've got a full musical disagreement happening."

Jess moved toward the door, heart full. "Are you coming?"

"Someone has to moderate that argument," he said, reaching for her hand.

She laced her fingers through his without hesitation, warmth blooming as their palms met.

Chapter Nineteen

Jessica

In the wake of the whirlwind that was Christmas morning—cocoa-fueled chaos, gifts half-unwrapped, tinsel trails left like breadcrumbs from breakfast to the parlor—Jess stepped out onto the back porch and took her first full breath of stillness.

Graham was already there, hands tucked into his jacket pockets, eyes tipped toward the treeline like he was watching for something in the snowfall.

The snow cloaked the world in a quiet white blanket, drifting lazily over the ridge in soft spirals by a gentle breeze. Pine trees stood tall and heavy all around the inn, their branches bowed and glittering—like even they were exhausted from the week's events.

He didn't speak. He shifted slightly, as if he could feel her standing behind him.

Jess pulled her coat tighter and slipped on the gloves she'd shoved in her back pocket. "You got a minute?"

Graham turned toward her, his mouth was already soft

with a smile. "For you?"

She raised an eyebrow. "If that's okay."

"Of course."

She grinned, and he stepped aside, nodding toward the trail that curved past the barn and down toward the small clearing tucked at the base of the ridge.

"I figure they've got about twenty minutes before the sugar wears off."

Jess exhaled a soft laugh. "Then let's take a walk before anyone realizes we've made a break for it."

The snow crunched beneath their boots; they both plodded along, not rushing. It was a silence that felt shared rather than empty. Peaceful. Earned.

For a little while, they walked in gentle rhythm—shoulders nearly touching, breath faintly visible in the cold morning air. Jess could hear the soft sound of music from the parlor window they had slipped away from: a half-finished carol fading as the needle skipped the last groove on the old record player. Someone would fix it. Not them.

"I keep thinking," Graham said finally, "how Margaret would've liked you."

Jess turned her head. "You do?"

He nodded slowly. "She loved people who made things feel lighter. That was her gift. I keep trying to do everything, and she just...knew which pieces mattered most."

Jess didn't respond right away. She took a few more steps before stopping near a frost-covered bench. Her boots squeaked softly as they crushed the fresh snow. "You were carrying her legacy, Graham. Your girls. This whole place."

He looked at her then—really looked. "I think for a long time, I thought I had to carry it alone."

Jess's eyes softened. She reached out, brushing a clump of snow from his coat sleeve. "You don't anymore."

He held her gaze. "I know. You've made sure I couldn't keep pretending."

They were quiet again, but this time the silence buzzed with something unspoken.

Then Jess lifted her chin, her words softer than before. "I didn't plan to care this much, you know. This week was supposed to be about rest. Laughing at other people's traditions. Cocoa with way too many marshmallows."

"That sounds about right." His voice dropped, warm and teasing. "Then you showed up like a holiday-themed hurricane and restructured half my emotional bandwidth."

That startled a laugh out of her—quick, bright.

"But," she added softly, "I care. About the girls. About you."

He stepped closer, not quite touching. "I didn't think I could feel like this again. Like my heart was waking up."

Jess's breath caught. "I don't want to make you feel like you're replacing Margaret."

"You're not," he said firmly. "You're here. Entirely yourself. And this is something new."

She looked up at him, her face tipped with wind-kissed color and something wide and open in her eyes. "Something unexpected, but good, right?"

"Yes," he said, barely louder than the wind.

Then he kissed her.

His hand gently supported her face, calloused thumb brushing her cheekbone as if she were something he never thought he'd get to hold again. She leaned in without hesitation, her fingers curling into the front of his jacket, anchoring herself as his mouth met hers.

The kiss was slow at first—careful, like reverence and memory combined into one breathless moment. It felt like he was giving himself permission to let go, and she was giving herself permission to take what she wanted. Neither of them had come this far for restraint.

She parted her lips, and he responded like gravity, deepening the kiss with a hunger that contradicted all the times he'd watched her laugh from across the room and not reached. Her pulse raced as his arms wrapped around her waist, pulling her close to him. There—finally, there—was the heat she'd only imagined. With his body firmly pressed against hers, the rasp of his stubble brushed her skin with every motion of the kiss.

He was warm and real and wrapped in flannel and cedar, and she melted into it like she'd been waiting for this kind of burn. She gasped softly, and he swallowed it—one arm sliding up her back, palm splayed between her shoulder blades, grounding and claiming her all at once.

He tasted like memory and something new—something wild and tender and full of a quiet longing, finally spoken out loud.

God, she wanted all of it.

Her hands moved upward, over solid shoulders and the nape of his neck, fingers tangling in slightly damp hair from the morning snow. He shivered slightly under her touch—but it was enough to send pleasure curling in her belly, tight and eager. She tilted her head, deepening the kiss, and he responded, mouth hot and possessive now, his control starting to slip.

The world blurred. The glow of Christmas lights flickered in her peripheral vision. Somewhere, a pine-scented candle sputtered. And, bringing it all together—him. Always him.

Every day leading up to this was filled with glances that lasted too long, hands brushing, promises woven into the way he said thank you, the way she passed him cocoa with no garnish, no questions.

He kissed her like someone who hadn't been kissed in too long. And she kissed him back like it had always been him.

When they finally broke apart, breath mingling in the small gap between them, he still held her close—his forehead resting against hers, their hearts beating wild and quiet in the same rhythm.

"I've wanted this," he whispered, voice low and rough.

"So have I." She nodded, still caught somewhere between gasp and prayer. "Do you have a cat?"

Startled by the abrupt change of topic, he stared at her. "Uh, no. The girls keep asking, but the chickens and twins are typically enough to keep me busy. Why?"

"Oh, just something a friend said." She thought about Candy. *You're going to come back with a fiancé and a cat.* No cat, but a girl could still dream.

His hand found hers again. Held it. Tangled it tight.

Neither of them let go.

Then—

"Daaaaad!"

Jess flinched against his chest just as Noelle's shout cut across the clearing like a flare.

"Where are you!?" Clara hollered. "Snow angel war begins at noon!"

They pulled back slowly, breathlessly.

Snowflakes clung to Graham's hair, melting along the scruff of his jaw where her gloved fingertips had just been. Jess stood in the hush between their bodies, eyelashes dusted white, lips parted. The ridge behind them fell quiet again, with only the faint rustle of wind threading through cedar boughs and the steady crunch of snow under their boots grounding them in the moment.

A crooked smile tugged at Graham's mouth as he leaned in, touching his forehead gently to hers. Their breaths mingled in the space between—warm and lingering, like neither could quite let go. Her hands rested flat against his chest, and his arms remained around her—not tightly, but like he was anchoring himself.

Jess looked up, eyes shining with something between mischief and emotion. She shifted just enough to tilt her chin, and Graham's grin flickered into something softer. Slower. They kissed again—curious and testing, finding the same heat that had simmered beneath the surface since the moment she'd first looked at him. His beard brushed against her lips, and she pulled him closer for a fraction of a second, then pushed him away. "They're coming."

A snowflake caught at the corner of her mouth as they parted, and he brushed it away with his thumb.

Then—voices and the scuff of boots over packed snow.

"Ewwwwwww!" Noelle shrieked from the top of the path, clutching a snowball with mittened hands and an expression of scandalized delight.

Clara groaned beside her, but the corner of her mouth tugged upward. "Literally two minutes. We left for two minutes."

Jess blinked, still breathless, laughing as she pressed a mitten to her mouth. Graham straightened slightly but didn't let go of Jess's waist.

"We were just—" Jess began.

"Kissing in the snow like a Hallmark movie couple," Noelle said loudly, clearly unimpressed. "We saw."

"I think it was romantic," Clara said more quietly, but still loud enough to make Jess laugh harder.

Graham tilted his head toward the girls. "Could've yelled a little sooner."

"Why?" Noelle shrugged. "You seemed to like it."

Jess wiped melted snow off her face, her hand still tucked in the warmth of Graham's. "We won't get in trouble with Santa, will we?"

Clara nodded solemnly. "Santa would approve, but Grandma might start planning a wedding."

Graham inhaled sharply—then chuckled. "Let's not start that conversation before lunch."

Noelle rolled her eyes. "Too late! We're telling everyone."

Jess squeezed his hand before slipping away to meet the girls on the path. Graham watched her go, red scarf loose around her shoulders, boots sinking slightly in the snow.

She looked back once.

He was still watching her, still smiling.

Mid-spin and full of mischief, Noelle announced, "Time to start the snow angel competition!"

"I get first pick!" Clara called.

Jess let out a half-laugh. "Snow angels?"

"I'm guessing there are rules," grumbled Graham.

Jess grinned and looked back up at him.

They'd pick it up later—this moment, this thread between them—but for now, they would play. Together.

Graham reached for her glove-clad hand and squeezed it, just once.

Her heart thudded.

"Let's go make snow angels," she whispered.

And then they ran, into the magic, into the snow, and toward something that felt dangerously like *more* than joy.

Chapter Twenty

Graham

The fire had burned low. It was just embers, glowing beneath a half-fallen log, but Graham stayed put. He sat on the leather chair closest to the hearth, his palms flat on his thighs, watching the quiet dance of orange and gold where flame met ash.

The parlor had emptied slowly after dinner, one guest at a time disappearing into doorways with murmured goodnights and sleepy smiles. The girls had gone last, with Clara barely making it down the hall and past the stairs without leaning on the wall, and Noelle asleep on her feet with chocolate still smudged behind one ear. He'd carried her the last few steps to their room.

Now, hours later, the inn had gone still.

He hadn't turned, blown out the candles, or turned off the tree's battery-operated lights. He couldn't. Beside him, the Santa mug someone had left near the hearth—half full of cooling cocoa—gave off the last bit of Christmas cheer for the day. The house was still heavy with a silent vibration, as if the walls were still holding the peals of laughter and crinkle of paper. The guests would leave in the coming days, and the usual surge of relief for things to go back to normal was missing.

He heard her before he saw her, footsteps in socks on the pinewood floors. The familiar shuffle of someone who wasn't sneaking but didn't want to wake the house.

Jess appeared from the hallway, her silhouette softened by the lamplight. She wore pajama pants—ivory with tiny gold stars—and an old Ladder H sweatshirt he'd seen her pull on a few times since she arrived. The cuffs covered her hands, and her hair was twisted into a careless style. She looked relaxed, but her eyes...they were sharp. Awake.

She crossed the room slowly.

"I thought you'd be asleep," she said, her voice just above a whisper.

He shook his head. "I didn't want it to end just yet."

She glanced at the fire, then back at him. "Me neither."

He pointed to the cushion beside him. "You staying up?"

Jess nodded and tucked herself next to him with quiet ease, one leg folded beneath her, the other brushing his knee as they settled. The fire cast a soft glow across the room, flickering against the framed doorways and the weave of the rug.

She glanced toward the tree. It was everything a tree should be—big, sparkling, and decorated with matching ornaments. It was nothing like the tree she'd put up with the girls, without lights and covered only in handmade ornaments that swung slightly as the girls ran by. She thought about the copper circle nestling just beneath a crooked red star, the ribbon catching and releasing the light.

"I've been thinking about your gift," she said, her voice quiet. "The ornament."

Graham turned slightly, arms resting on his thighs.

Jess watched the firelight dance across his profile. "You made it for me."

The pause dragged on, long, but not uncertain. Just be careful. "Yeah," he said. "I did."

Jess looked down at her lap, where her hand rested. Her fingers were still lightly smudged with the glitter that refused to leave her skin, sparkling souvenirs from a day full of laughter with the girls.

"It felt honest," she said. "Like you weren't trying to say everything. Just...something."

Graham exhaled, slow and quiet. "Honestly, Jess, you deserve so much more than that."

She turned toward him again. The fire popped once, soft and unimposing.

Her voice dropped. "It meant something, Graham. Like more than anything I've gotten this year. Probably more than anything I've gotten in a long time."

Silence settled around the room again, but this one wasn't heavy. It was warm. Like the fire—low and steady, no longer asking for attention, just giving it.

He swallowed, then said. "I didn't expect you," he said. "Not like this."

Her brow rose slightly, but it wasn't in surprise. "What do you mean?"

Graham ran a thumb along the inside of his palm. "I thought the parts of me that could feel something like this were behind me. I've been so focused on surviving the holidays that I didn't realize...I stopped living in them."

She reached out, her fingers brushing his where his hand rested on his knee. "You haven't stopped, Graham. You pour love into every single person that walks through that door."

"I pour effort," he said, bitter around the edges. "I never thought anyone would notice the difference." He looked up at her, voice low. "But you do."

She didn't flinch or fill the silence with a gentle platitude. She simply nodded once and softly said, "Grief makes you hold your breath too long, and then life sneaks in when you aren't watching."

He stared at her hand on top of his. "And now?"

Jess shrugged. "Now I think we're both starting to exhale."

The fire cracked, with a soft pop.

He moved his hand slowly—so she could pull away if she chose—and curled his fingers around hers. She didn't move.

"I want to kiss you," he said plainly.

She blinked, then tilted her head, exposing the pull at the corner of her mouth.

"Then kiss me," she said.

So, he did.

His hand cradled her face, thumb gentle along her jaw. When their lips met, it wasn't a collision. It was slow and steady—a promise rather than a plunge. She leaned into it almost immediately, lips parting, hand sliding up to lightly curl around the collar of his sweatshirt. He deepened the kiss instinctively, with emotion rushing beneath every inch of contact—so long unnamed, suddenly unmistakable.

When they pulled back, neither moved far. Both hesitant to create more space between their bodies, their breath still mingled and shared.

"This is real," she whispered.

"I know."

Her brow furrowed slightly. Vulnerable, but unshielded now. "I don't want to make assumptions. But I want you to know I'm here. Like really here."

He closed his eyes briefly, then opened them again and looked at her, soul bare.

"I want you, Jess," he murmured, voice rough as new snow underfoot. "In a way, I didn't think I'd ever be allowed to want someone again."

She didn't look away. Her eyes shimmered in the gentle glow of the parlor light, reflecting a mix of surprise and certainty, as if she'd been hoping he'd say it but also feared it.

With a gentle touch, she caressed his jaw, her thumb grazing the patch of stubble just beneath his cheekbone. "So do I," she said, her voice a tender exhale more than speech.

Graham's throat worked through emotion, and for just a second, he pressed his forehead against hers, grounding himself in her presence and the steadiness of her breath. Her gloved fingers intertwined with his. They were firm, sure, anchoring him to the present—a present he hadn't allowed himself to believe in for years.

"I forgot how this feels," he admitted, his mouth brushing her temple as he spoke. "Wanting something this much. Not just..." His free hand slid up her waist, past her ribs, along the fabric of her coat, fingertips tracing a line so whisper-soft it made her whole body come alive.

"Not just wanting," he finished. "Craving."

Jess drew back slowly, enough to see the look in his eyes. To let him see the heat in hers.

Then she pulled him back into a kiss, and there was no hesitation this time. No caution.

Just hunger.

His lips met hers in a deep sweep, pulling her closer. The frigid air that had settled between them vanished with a flash of heat. His hands slipped beneath her coat, wrapping around her waist and spreading wide across her back. Jess parted her lips with a soft gasp, inviting him in. He accepted the gesture and deepened the kiss, gently coaxing rather than demanding, yet it still left her dizzy.

Jess pressed into him, hands curling into his shirt as their bodies moved closer, hips angling, heat pooling low and fast. Her fingers slid up under the soft fabric of his collar, brushing his bare neck. He groaned into her mouth and walked her backward, slow and sure, until her back hit the wall beside the archway. He bracketed her there with his body, shielding her from everything that wasn't snow and pulse and promise.

"I can't stop thinking…" His voice was husky now, rough with longing. His fingers traced the curve of her waist. "About what you feel like under all these layers. About touching you.. .really touching you."

The words slammed into her, hot and honest, and Jess whimpered softly at the way he said it. Not crude…*reverent*.

A knot of heat twisted low in her belly. Jess was already panting, breath shallow, fingers dragging up the front of his shirt until they fit into the space between his buttons, sliding softly against warm skin.

"I want it, too," she breathed, brushing her lips along his jaw. "I want you in my bed. Your hands on me. The weight of your body...everything."

He let out something between a growl and a prayer, catching her mouth again, mouth firmer now.

And this kiss...this kiss wasn't soft.

It was every missed moment, every held breath, every ache that had built over days of almosts and not-quites. His hand slid down to her thigh, gently pulled her leg between his, fitting her to him, letting her feel just how much he burned for her.

She gasped against his mouth.

Then, his lips hovered just above hers. When he spoke, his breath brushed her skin, trembling through her bones.

"Tell me to follow you," he said.

Jess blinked slowly, the heat rising all the way to her throat. "I'm going upstairs," she said softly. "To my room."

She slid her fingers slowly along his jaw, her chest rising and falling. "And after you check on the girls, if you want to come up..."

Her eyes never left his.

"The door will be open."

She kissed him once more—deliberate and full of promise—then turned toward the stairwell, every step slow, aching with invitation.

And Graham?

He stood there for a heartbeat longer, heart thundering in his chest.

His stomach did something quiet and unfamiliar. Twisting, anticipating.

"Okay," he said.

Jess leaned forward and kissed him once more—slow, gentle, just mouth against mouth—and then slid her fingers away from his with a final squeeze.

She stood without looking back.

After she disappeared around the corner, Graham sat with his elbows on his knees, staring at the logs that had burned almost to ash.

Then he blew out his breath and stood, heart thudding as he walked quietly down the hall.

To check the doors.

To make sure the girls were sound asleep.

And to decide whether tonight was the beginning of something he hadn't let himself believe in...until now.

Chapter Twenty-One

Jessica

She waited.

Outside her window, snow drifted gently across the glass panes—silent flurries melting into darkness—while inside, Jess sat cross-legged on the bed, blanket loosely wrapped around her waist, her heart beating unevenly.

Graham hadn't come yet.

Of course, it had only been a few minutes since she slipped away from the parlor, but every second felt longer than the last. She looked at the brass key on the nightstand as if it might hold an answer. The room was warm. With the wind softly gusting outside the window, the battery-operated lamp cast a pale light over her neatly folded flannel pajamas.

It probably should have felt silly, waiting like this. But nothing about tonight felt silly.

Jess stood, exhaled slowly, and moved to her suitcase. She unzipped the top just enough to reach for the soft folds she had tucked away days earlier. Her fingers touched the flannel pajamas Taylor helped her choose. Crisp, red, and butter-soft, the kind meant to be worn barefoot on a snowy morning. She held the button-up top in her hands, brushing the hem where the tag still rustled faintly.

And then...the box.

Small. White. Untied.

Taylor had slid it into her bag as she left Houston, with a wink and zero explanation.

Jess opened it now. Inside was a note, written in Taylor's looping script: *A little reminder that you're allowed to feel beautiful.*

Next to the note was a pair of red lace panties, delicate as a spiderweb, elegant, and unapologetic. Wholly inadequate for warmth.

Feminine and sure. Like Taylor had known somehow, what Jess wouldn't admit out loud—a girl needed a little help to feel special sometimes.

She smiled slowly and a little breathlessly.

Sliding her arms into the flannel shirt, she fastened only three buttons. Just enough to look decent, but still honest. The matching shorts sat low on her hips, the hem brushing the tops of her thighs, with the red lace panties showing at the waist.

She padded back to the bed and sat on the edge of the mattress, back straight, blanket pooled at her side.

Her heart thudded steadily beneath the flannel.

She thought about Candy, wide-eyed and laughing. *You're gonna come back with a fiancé and a cat.*

And Taylor, calmly folding winter layers into her suitcase. *If it feels good—let it. You don't always have to fight for peace.*

She didn't know what tonight meant, but she knew there was no cat.

There was a knock at the door so soft she almost missed it.

She stood before she could talk herself out of it and opened the door.

Graham.

He filled the doorway in flannel and flurries. Snow speckled his sweater, and a hint of smoke and chilly air clung to him. His hair was damp around the temples. His eyes locked on hers, then drifted downward—wide, reverent—until a slow smile tugged across his lips.

"That flannel won't do much to keep you warm."

"Well, I was hoping you'd help with that." Jess's smile tipped and turned into something more playful. "I thought I'd give in to local customs."

His grin deepened. "That's not local," he said quietly, stepping inside. "That's just perfect."

The door clicked shut.

He stood still, like she might vanish if he moved too fast.

Jess approached him slowly, keeping her eyes on his. When her fingers brushed his chest, they paused for half a second before tightening her grasp on the soft knit of his sweater.

Their connection grounded both of them in the moment.

"You came," she whispered, not as a question but as a quiet acknowledgment of something neither of them had said aloud until now.

"I wasn't going to miss this," he answered. The words were low and rough, more gravel than breath, but steady as a promise. He seemed to leave something unsaid, and she finished his unspoken thought. *Especially if tonight is the only night we get to hold each other.*

She tipped her chin up. He didn't rush. Just looked—really looked—as if he was taking in every inch of her: the flush blooming high on her cheeks, the softness in her gaze, the way her breath hitched when he stepped closer and thumbed the edge of her sleeve.

Their kiss began softly—hesitant, almost shy. It deepened only enough to tell the truth they'd both been avoiding.

When they parted, he rested his forehead against hers. "Tell me if this is too fast," he murmured.

"It's not," she breathed. "I just—needed to know what this was."

His thumb brushed her cheek. "It's real," he said simply.

She smiled, tears threatening.

"You're so beautiful," he said simply.

"Graham."

"This feels like a Christmas miracle."

"Jess..." He said it as if it were a prayer, then he reached to turn down the lamp, leaving only the faint glow of snow light spilling across the floor. The room felt smaller, quieter, wrapped in a stillness that held its own kind of promise.

"I haven't felt this steady...this wanted...in years."

"You are," he said immediately, his voice thick and low with truth. "I want you...this...us..."

They kissed again, pulling each other closer.

In the quiet hours that followed, they drifted in and out. No rush. No distance. Just presence and relief, with hands that lingered and breaths that matched and hearts that, somehow, beat easier now.

Like everything, they'd been holding on to something that finally had space to let go. And in the hush of snow and firelight, they let it.

Sometimes Jess would wake just to find him watching her, the pad of his thumb tracing her wrist, like her pulse underneath his touch was proof enough that this was real.

When morning light finally crept past the frost-trimmed window, Jess stirred.

Graham's arm stayed tucked beneath her neck, his other resting over her ribs. She turned toward him, lips grazing his collarbone.

"Good morning," she whispered.

He didn't open his eyes. Just smiled. "Already is."

She exhaled, soft and sure.

This was no longer a holiday escape.

This was something they'd have to name. Build. Choose. But for now, it was enough that his body was wrapped around hers and holding her there.

Chapter Twenty-Two

Jessica

The bed was still warm when Graham slipped quietly out from under the quilt.

The faint light of early dawn filtered through the frost-covered window, painting the Juniper Room with a blue-gray calm. Jess stirred but didn't wake—her breathing slow and steady, dark curls spread across the pillow like ink on snow. One hand rested near where his chest had been, fingers curled loosely, as if still holding onto him in her dreams.

He gazed at her for a long moment, her heartbeat steady. She looked beautiful like this—soft and sleeping. A part of him wanted to stay, to wrap himself around her again, and fall back into that lazy, dream-soft place where everything was want and warmth.

But the girls would be up soon.

It wasn't shame that pushed him from the bed—it was discretion. The choice a dad makes when he's falling in love but still has a hallway full of holiday magic to protect.

He leaned down once, brushing a kiss across her bare shoulder, just above the red flannel sheet she hadn't pulled back up.

Then he slipped out.

Jess woke to light streaming across the bed. She blinked slowly into the emptiness beside her, hand sliding over the warm spot Graham had left behind.

The quilt was tucked around her. Her shirt had slipped off during the early hours, but the blanket had been pulled over her as if he had made sure she was covered before they left.

She smiled.

Soft. *Full.*

Not the dreamy grin of fleeting joy, but something deeper. Without rushing, she stretched and stood, pulling a throw off the bed and wrapping it around her.

Her body was still warm with his hands, his breath, the way he'd whispered her name somewhere between the star-studded night and his departure at sunrise.

She ran a hand through her hair, scooped her flannel top from the floor, and tugged it over bare skin. Then, she padded barefoot into the hallway.

The inn was awake.

A warm, familiar laugh drifted from downstairs. Her steps quickened.

As she neared the kitchen, the scent hit her first.

Maple syrup. Toasted muffins. Crispy bacon and something vaguely citrusy—maybe marmalade? It all mingled with wood smoke and the faint vanilla scent of leftover cookies. She pressed her palm to the wall, her heart adjusting.

Inside, the girls chattered at full tilt.

Clara sat perched on a stool at the island, reading a recipe card and precisely timing her dad's egg-flipping. Noelle danced in socks across the tile, tossing fruit peels into the compost bin and occasionally sprinkling cinnamon sugar over buttered toast—most of it ending up on the bread.

And in the middle of it all was Graham.

Hair damp, sleeves rolled, barefoot in jeans and a threadbare Henley stretched over broad shoulders. He was humming. Actually humming. A low, tuneless thread beneath the sound of sizzling batter and giggling girls.

Jess stood in the doorway, lingered, and let it all sink in.

Graham, standing at the stove, caught her eye over his shoulder. Across the expanse of a kitchen that had seen a lifetime of mornings, in that instant, the noise and hustle faded away.

Something unspoken passed between them: quiet recognition, the bittersweet ache of endings and beginnings at the same time. She held his gaze, and the entire world shrank into that flooded, golden space between them. They didn't need words. The truth sat silently between them, anyway. The power was back, the holiday magic still lingered, but real life—her departure, responsibilities, longing—was slowly creeping back in.

"Morning," she whispered.

Clara swiveled on her stool. "You're awake! Finally!"

"We didn't want to wake you," Noelle said, already elbow-deep in a bowl of pancake batter, sleeves pushed to her elbows and glitter stuck to the corner of one eyebrow. "But the power's back on! Daddy started the water heater already, and I made toast in the actual toaster, not parlor fire toast."

Jess grinned as she stepped into the kitchen, savoring the aroma of sugar and cinnamon, the sizzle and simmer of breakfast in motion, and all the soft, ordinary music of a *home*.

"We're making pancakes," Clara added firmly. "With chocolate chips and marshmallow swirl, and you have to layer the toppings. Mixing them in is incorrect."

Jess brought a hand to her chest, mock solemn. "Of course. A chef must honor the pancake creed."

Graham turned back to the skillet and flipped a perfect golden circle onto a rising stack. "Hungry?" he asked over his shoulder.

Jess's glance caught the full spread laid out beside him. There was fruit in a ceramic bowl, whipped cinnamon butter softening in a snowflake-shaped dish, tiny ramekins of warm syrup and cream. The gold-rimmed plates were mismatched, and the napkins were gently wrinkled. It didn't matter that the tablecloth wasn't ironed or that the mugs didn't match because the room glowed.

It felt extraordinary because the ordinary parts mattered most.

It was comfort without ceremony.

It was the rhythm of a household, not polished, but practiced.

Graham turned and nodded toward a sun-warmed stool at the corner of the island. "We saved you a seat."

Jess eased into it. The wood was smooth from wear, and the seat tilted ever so slightly to the left. The kitchen buzzed around her quietly, alive with morning joy.

She looked down at her hands, then over at Graham as he reached for a clean plate and slid it toward her.

Her heart thumped. Was it always this simple?

"I like this," she murmured.

Graham didn't speak. Just reached across the island and laid his hand gently over hers. His thumb traced a slow arc, not demanding anything, just anchoring her there, now.

A promise without punctuation.

Noelle leaned in, eyes sparkling behind her purple-rimmed glasses. "Daddy said maybe we could make lasagna together tonight."

Clara nodded, fanning herself with a paper menu she'd made from a half-colored placemat. "If we use the big pan, it'll make enough for lunch tomorrow, too."

Jess's throat tightened. Not with sadness, but with something gentler. The beginnings of an invitation.

"I'll show you how to layer the noodles and break the eggs for the filling with just one hand," she said, smiling over the rim of her mug and looked around again at the stove, the girls now arguing playfully over topping distribution ratios, the dappled light filtering through the old kitchen curtains, and the curl of Graham's smile.

The realization sank in. He never needed saving; he just needed help. Someone to share the routines of regular mornings—extra hands in warm dish water, someone to wash felted socks while padding across pine floors, an extra voice laughing at breakfast, and maybe, they needed her.

Jess lifted her fork but paused for a fleeting second to let the moment stretch.

She let herself imagine staying.

Staying in this kitchen. In its warmth. In its mess.

Spending early Tuesday mornings with toast and science fair anxiety. On Friday nights, amidst glitter jars and floor-fort kingdoms, with bedtimes 30 minutes past usual.

Staying in the comforting knowledge that this life didn't expect perfection from her. It didn't need flawless plans or best-foot-forward charm. Only that she show up brave, a little unsure, entirely human.

Jess looked at Graham's hands resting on the butcher block, fingers splayed wide, his thumb tracing slow, absent loops. She thought about how he held her hand the night before, pulling her close to create a simple connection. It was still something that needed to be named.

And the girls...

God, the girls.

Clara raised one eyebrow in her overly serious way, trying to act like a grown-up, her brows furrowed as she watched the syrup pour. Her braid was fuzzy from sleep.

Noelle, wild-haired and syrup-slicked, leaned her cheek against Jess's shoulder in a flash of affection—just a beat, maybe two—and slipped away again without saying anything. No explanation. No big deal. Just trust. That cheek press carried a weight of something larger than it looked.

This wasn't just a holiday escape.

This wasn't an imagined joy.

This wasn't temporary.

It was the start of imperfect mornings and glitter disasters and the way someone's palm can anchor you with nothing more than presence.

Something quietly spectacular.

And something she didn't want to leave behind.

Chapter Twenty-Three

Jessica

With a quick zip, Jess closed her suitcase and carried it down the narrow back staircase.

She had packed her sweaters, snow globe, and red flannel pajamas. Carefully repacking each item, her fingers gently folded and tucked as if to stretch time just a little longer. It felt incredibly tender, holding such real memories for something she hadn't planned or expected, but now couldn't imagine not carrying with her.

The thought of her time with Graham in the Juniper Room weighed heavily on her. She couldn't erase the memory of his hands on her waist, the stillness of the night, the slow drift of breath against shared pillows. Jess quietly closed the suitcase, letting the latch click shut with a sound far too final for what this felt like.

This was all new to her. She hadn't slept with anyone watching the snow fall outside her window before, hadn't kissed a man who made her laugh and ache in equal measure, and hadn't sat on a threadbare window seat and wished—really wished—for something she wanted to come back to...and now she was leaving.

For now.

The inn softly said its goodbyes—the familiar floor creak outside the parlor, the warm maple aroma still lingering faintly in the hallway, the tiny smear of cocoa powder beside the kettle where Noelle had tried (and failed) to refill it alone.

Outside, the world sparkled white.

The air had a sharp brightness that only follows a winter storm—sun-glint bouncing off the windows of the upper rooms, and icicles hanging stubbornly from the porch eaves like teeth. Melt pooled in shallow dents of water on the driveway, and slow streams threaded down the gravel in ribbons. Absolute stillness in the deep pines, their boughs were heavy and bowed with snow.

The porch creaked under Jess's footsteps as she stepped out, dragging her worn duffel behind her. She paused for a moment on the top step, her shoulders hunched beneath her wool coat and let the cold bite her cheeks and fill her lungs.

Below her, waiting beside the parked rental car, stood Graham.

He hadn't heard her yet. One gloved hand rested on the hood of the vehicle; his head was slightly ducked as he wiped something from the corner of the windshield. His cheeks were pink, and his breath puffed out in soft clouds as he moved. The sleeves of his flannel were rolled up to his forearms again—she thought of it as his 'get-stuff-done' uniform—revealing his chapped knuckles and strong wrists. He had already scraped the windshield and shoveled out a path for her.

There was glitter on his sleeve.

Of course, there was.

Jess smiled.

As if sensing her watching, he turned.

Their eyes met.

His smile wasn't wide. It never was. But it was deep and quiet. It was a smile that said: *I see you. I'll miss you. This doesn't end here.*

He straightened and crossed the gravel with purpose. It wasn't fast or dramatic, but sure. He wasn't trying to hold her there or rush her off. He let her set the pace.

"You sure about this car?" he asked, nodding to the rental.

Jess gave him a mock frown. "Worried it won't make it down the hill?"

"I just doubt it can clear a snowbank and still stay on the road," he said, tugging one last smear of melted frost off the bumper. Then, softer: "You're packed?"

She nodded. Her voice caught for a moment, so she simply tapped the duffel by her side. "Ornament, snow globe, flannel, lace..."

He reached forward, brushing a curl from her cheek with the back of his fingers. "And you remembered your charger?"

"Yeah, I'm already leaving enough behind," she whispered.

He rested his palm against her waist then, warm even through her coat. "The girls wrote out rules for how often you have to call," he said. "They debated texting but then concluded you were a 'sentence person.'"

"I'll take that as a compliment."

"Hey," he said suddenly, tipping her chin gently so she couldn't look anywhere but at him. The air between them shifted—intimate, charged with all the things they weren't ready to say. "You're coming back."

She didn't flinch. "Yes."

"Promise?"

Jess leaned into him then, fingers clutching the front of his coat, anchoring herself in the warmth he carried even as the cold pressed in around them. Her forehead came to rest against his chest—just briefly—but long enough to memorize the steady beat of his heart beneath soft flannel and the layers of a man who didn't offer comfort lightly.

A gust of wind swirled snow gently around them, catching in their hair and clinging to the folds of their coats.

"I'm not done with this story, Graham Walker," she whispered.

His exhale was quiet, deep. When he wrapped his arms around her, it wasn't with urgency or farewell; it was slow and deliberate. His hands pressed the small of her back, fitting their bodies together, pulling her in close without tightening.

"I warmed it up for you," he said, nodding toward the car.

"Any ice left on those back roads?"

"Some," he said. "But less than yesterday." He hesitated. "Still wouldn't mind if you waited until it melts completely and stayed another night."

Jess smiled. "Tempting. Very tempting."

His mouth quirked, but he didn't push.

The back door squealed open, and the twins burst out in matching winter coats and slightly mismatched boots. Clara held a lumpy paper envelope with Jess's name written carefully across the flap. Noelle carried a gingerbread cookie badly taped into a paper towel.

"This is for you," Clara said, offering the envelope. "It's an adventure map."

"It's so you don't get lost on the way back," Noelle added. "Because Dad says the GPS is a liar."

Jess crouched to their height, doing her best not to cry as she accepted both gifts. "Well, I feel safer already."

"You'll come back, right?" Clara asked, eyes too old and too hopeful.

Jess glanced at Graham, then back at them. "Yes. As soon as I can."

"You could just stay," Noelle said smartly.

"Subtle," Graham muttered.

"I'd like that," Jess said. "But I have patients counting on me. That's important."

Noelle leaned in like she had a secret. "You could have patients here instead."

Jess hugged them both so tightly that Clara squeaked, and Noelle yelled dramatically, then giggled as she hugged them even tighter.

When Jess finally stepped back, Graham had already loaded her bags into the trunk. She walked around the car and opened the driver's side door.

And stopped.

Jess stared at him then, really stared—at the crinkle of snow near his boots, the way his beard caught the winter light, how he stood like he wasn't sure if this was the moment she kissed him or said goodbye forever.

She stepped closer. Reached for his jacket lapels with a surety that bypassed doubt.

His breath left him in puffs of cold air.

Her fingers curled into the soft-scrubbed flannel beneath his coat. Her eyes searched his.

"That was the single most amazing Christmas I've ever had," she whispered.

He finally looked up. "Holly House has a reputation—"

"Stop," she whispered."

She leaned up and kissed him.

Slow. Sure.

The kind of kiss that said thank you, and something more: *I'm not ready to say goodbye.*

When she pulled back, Graham breathed deep, swallowed thick.

"You still have my number?" he asked quietly, voice roughened.

"I have more than that," she said.

Then, with one last look—over the snow-banked road, back at the twins waving from the porch, toward the ridge beginning to lose its light—she smiled.

"I'll be back."

Finally, reluctantly, she stepped back a breath and wiped a stray snowflake from his beard with the soft edge of her glove. Her fingers lingered.

"See you soon," she said, her voice just above a whisper.

He nodded, unable to trust himself to speak, his face warm and full. She could see it in his eyes: he wasn't going to stop her from leaving, but he wasn't going to close the door between them either.

Jess adjusted her scarf, looping it twice before slipping into the driver's seat. She pulled the car door closed with a muted click. Then, she sat for a moment with her hands on the steering wheel, staring out through the windshield, still slightly fogged by the car's heat.

After a deep breath, she pulled off her gloves and reached instinctively for the seat belt. But paused.

Something shimmered in the cupholder beside her.

A small flash of copper, catching the late morning sun through the windshield.

She stilled.

Then smiled—eyes glassy, chest squeezed tight—as her fingers closed around the familiar cool weight of the ornament he had made.

HOLLY HOUSE, the etched front read, glowing with a warm, handmade luster like it had soaked in all the memories the week had held.

She turned it over.

May you find a life filled with the same joy you've given us.—G

She laughed, but it folded in on itself, catching in her throat with a breath that almost turned to tears. She leaned forward, forehead settling gently against the steering wheel, one hand still closed around the ornament's edge.

A few tears welled, but she didn't let them fall. Just breathed them back. In. Out. Slowly.

Outside the window, Graham stood exactly where she'd left

him, with his hands in his coat pockets. She imagined his fists clenched, resisting the urge to stop her.

The snow swirled around him in loose spirals, settling on his shoulders and sparking the cuffs of his jeans. The porch steps behind him shimmered, dappled with sunlight filtering through cirrus clouds.

He smiled at her.

Not a wave. Not a reach. Just that knowing, quiet smile that had lived at the corner of his mouth all week—deeper now with understanding. A promise held steady from a man who didn't say things he didn't mean.

And Jess exhaled, palm resting on the ornament in her lap.

She felt steady.

Grounded.

Not because their goodbye had gotten easier.

But what they'd created here—the moment, the memory, the possibility—was never meant to be stored away neatly in a bag or wrapped up in a text thread. It didn't belong to borrowed days or cozy holiday illusions.

It was bigger.

Braver.

And it was *theirs.*

Then, without second-guessing it, she stepped out of the car.

The cold air kissed her cheeks immediately, pinching her bare fingers.

"I needed one more squeeze before letting you go," she said, walking toward him.

"As many as you need, for as long as you want," he replied,

voice low, as if he was trying not to crack anything between them.

She stepped forward, a soft smile tugging at the corner of her mouth, and slid her arms slowly around his waist. Her head was tucked just beneath his chin. His arms came around her on instinct. The hug wasn't desperate. It wasn't dramatic. It was reverent.

Jess pulled back slowly, fingers lingering at the opening of his coat.

"This is the best kind of impossible." Her voice caught a little. A wry, wondering smile curved up around it.

Graham reached for her face. One hand, careful but certain, cupped her cheek, his thumb grazing away the single tear that she'd been unable to hold back.

"No," he said simply, brushing a curl away from her temple. "This is real."

She nodded wordlessly, leaned into his touch, then let go.

Returning to the car was harder the second time.

She gripped the steering wheel as she climbed in and blinked once to refocus.

As she turned the key, the engine reluctantly hummed to life. Heat slowly pushed through the vents, and the windshield wipers cleared the increasingly heavy dusting of snow.

Noelle bounced with her hands waving like flags. Clara rested her chin on her arms against the patio railing, smiling with the kind of knowing solemnity that only an old soul could carry at eight years old.

Jess raised her hand. A quiet wave. Not goodbye, but a promise to see them again soon.

A few paces below the porch, Graham raised his too, the lines at the edges of his eyes creasing softly.

She caught his gaze one last time.

Then she shifted the car into gear and eased forward.

Her tires crunched over powdery gravel, with the trees arching overhead as the road curved away from the porch. The world stretched out in front of her—back toward Serenity, her clinic, and her life.

And maybe, move forward into something even better.

With her pulse steady and the sky expanding ahead, she drove east—carrying the memory of a cocoa-fueled Christmas, two yin and yang girls, and the slow, deliberate promise of Graham Walker resting inside her.

Chapter Twenty-Four

Jessica

Her home looked just as she had left it—quiet, tidy, and faintly illuminated by the afternoon sun filtering through west-facing windows. Jess closed the door behind her, her shoulder pressing against it briefly as if bracing for impact. Her suitcase softly thudded by the hall closet. She didn't bother unpacking.

The faint perfume of fake cinnamon still lingered in the air from the candle she'd burned before leaving for Cedar Glen. It no longer smelled right—funny how memory clings to the little things. On the kitchen counter, her grocery list was still tucked under a magnet next to an unopened envelope from her insurance provider. The dish rack hadn't moved. A single mug remained by the sink. The foundation of her daily life, untouched through the world's longest and shortest week.

Despite the unchanged surroundings, she stood in her home feeling like a different person entirely.

She crossed to the couch and placed her keys in the bowl next to the mail. Her coat slipped from her shoulders and landed on the arm of the chair she had always meant to reupholster. A week ago, she was curled up in that very spot, wrapped in cotton pajamas, with her laptop on her knees, scouring holiday retreats with a desperation she hadn't been willing to name aloud.

A week ago, she'd been trying to escape the ache of being left behind.

Now, she was carrying warmth so deeply rooted in her chest it felt like a spark born into flame.

Jess moved toward the seat by the window and sank down slowly, her eyes drifting over the familiar view of downtown Serenity. The buildings still wore garland, and the crisp winter air still chilled the glass. Bailey would've already taken Rosie to see the lights strung across the bakery awning. Candy was probably elbow-deep in sugar before sunrise. Jackson was probably rocking his baby to sleep or holding Molly's hand in the quiet home that now belonged to their growing family.

He'd messaged her on Christmas Day to tell her that the Beaumont family had a new addition. At 2:03 a.m., they'd welcomed Olivia Rose into the world. During Molly's pregnancy, Jess had wondered how it would feel to get that news. Sometimes, on her darkest days, she'd worry that letting Jackson go had been one of the biggest mistakes of her life. Now, she knew she'd done the right thing, and the best was yet to come.

She pressed her hand against the tug in her chest.

This was still her hometown, still her life, but the ache of what was missing wasn't as strong anymore. It had quieted, softened behind the memory of two glitter-covered girls and one man whose silence had made room for everything honest and real she'd forgotten she deserved.

Her gaze shifted to the small pile of mail.

She'd been caring for others' needs so long, she nearly forgot how it felt to take care of herself.

A soft smile crept onto Jess's face as she pulled her phone out of her coat pocket, the cool metal touching her fingertip. She curled her legs underneath her and leaned into the seat cushion. Outside, the rooftops of downtown Serenity shimmered in the late afternoon light.

She unlocked her phone and opened her notes app. A half-finished to-do list waited for her. It felt like a ghost from a life measured by urgency and routine. *Order flu vaccines. Staff meeting at 10. Call maintenance about the heat.*

Tasks she'd once approached with clinical precision now blurred, like she'd been focused on solving the wrong problems and answering the wrong questions.

Jess sat straighter. She inhaled—slow and deep—letting the air stretch through her ribcage like she was trying to make space where new dreams might fit. A cloud slowly rolled past, shifting the sun's angle through the windowpane. She felt its warmth across the right side of her face, casting long slats of light across her living room floor, striping her boots, her suitcase. Her life paused.

Then, slowly—deliberately—she opened a new list.

She wanted to put her thoughts and feelings into order...how could she say: *I'm choosing this?*

She shifted, thumb hovering over the keyboard, then began.

Open clinic hiring packet.

The words blinked up at her. She hadn't dared to consider

it seriously before. Not really. But now? It didn't feel like a failure. Delegating wasn't giving up. Delegating was giving herself room—to breathe, to build something bigger than what burned her out.

She chewed the tip of her thumbnail, then typed her next note.

Reach out to Dr. Moore and ask if she's ready for a part-time schedule.

She imagined Dr. Moore's calm demeanor, her unshakable patience during flu season, her quiet yet capable presence in the exam rooms. Jess had trained her in language, systems, and bedside manner. She was a perfect example of someone who could step in and keep the clinic's heartbeat going.

But Jess had never offered Dr. Moore that chance, because for years, she'd been so afraid that stepping back meant walking away.

Her eyes fixed on her old stethoscope hanging over the back of the kitchen stool. Even from here, she could see the faint wear on the tubing, and the name tag curling slightly at the edges.

It didn't speak of quitting.

It spoke of a legacy ready to be shared.

She tapped the screen of her phone gently, then added:

Call admin about interviewing a new nurse manager.

Her thumb hovered again.

The thought used to terrify her.

Hiring meant trust. Trust meant allowing someone else to see the chaos, the mess, the parts of the clinic that weren't glossy brochures and community awards. It meant vulnerability. But lately, the idea of sharing the burden didn't feel dangerous.

It felt like hope. Like sustainability. Like living beyond the next crisis.

Jess swallowed hard.

She could almost hear Candy's voice beside her, low and affectionate. "Let someone help you, Jess. You don't always have to be the emergency contact."

She smiled at that and typed:

Review savings. Again.

A pause. A breath.

Her heel tapped against the hardwood rhythmically as she did the math in her head—the money she'd socked away for just-in-case, for unexpected repairs, for the kind of life she now realized maybe she didn't want to fix anymore. Maybe, she wanted to reshape it instead.

The money wasn't endless, but it was enough.

Enough to shift a few things.

To hire part-time help.

To get someone else on the books.

To take a few weeks next season—spring, maybe—to head back. See if something like a doctor-on-the-ridge was more than just a dream induced by copper and flannel.

She glanced out the window again and watched a child walking their dog in a red puffer coat down Main Street. The leash trailed behind. All she wanted was to go back. To table games and bunk beds and morning cocoa with cinnamon dust floating lazily atop.

She dipped her chin. Let her eyes slip closed for a moment. Then typed one more line:

Give yourself permission to want more than this.

And under it, soft and certain:

Start.

That was it. Not a to-do, not a deadline. Just the click of something real.

Not an escape plan.

A homeward one.

Pack essentials—only essentials. (Also, bring glitter-free soap?)

A laugh escaped her unfiltered. That one was for Noelle—who somehow had turned every surface of the inn (and Jess's soul, if she were being honest) into a snow-dusted diorama of joyful chaos. Clara would have written out a clean packing checklist—Jess could almost see it now in her carefully printed lines.

Her chest tugged gently.

Then she typed:

Make room for the impossible.

For a long beat, she stared.

Those five words were on her screen, waiting.

So much of her life had been about controlling the outcome. Organizing into place. Fixing, managing, refining—always in motion. But Cedar Glen had taught her something quieter: the value of the unplanned, the unimagined, the sort of magic you didn't pencil in, but welcomed when it arrived in boots and flannel and a quiet, heart-altering steadiness.

Her thumb hovered, then pressed return.

One more line.

Return to Holly House.

She typed it slowly. The moment she finished the sentence,

the breath she'd been holding released in a quiet rush. Her lungs expanded like they hadn't fully expanded since before she'd left for the ridge.

Jess leaned back and tilted her head until it lightly tapped the glass. Outside, the last streaks of sunlight touched the edges of rooftops. Inside, her apartment remained its cozy, curated silence, but her body no longer felt the need for it. Her mind didn't need to soften against it because she was no longer fleeing from noise.

She was walking toward something.

Something bright and messy. Something filled with frosting-stained napkins, late-night puzzle battles, and the feel of Graham's palm across the small of her back, as if she belonged right there.

Cedar Glen had started as an escape—that part was true—but it had ended as a turning point.

She didn't want to "get away" anymore.

She wanted to build something softer. Something slower.

With girls who made her laugh…and a man who had handed her his heart one quiet gesture at a time.

She closed her eyes.

Inside her suitcase, she had carefully placed the copper ornament in the side pocket. Its inscription was warm, and its wish was undeniable.

May you find a life filled with the same joy you've given us.—G

Jess opened her eyes again. She was ready to stop worrying that this was a goodbye and start believing it could be her happy ending. One written with snowflakes, second chances, and a simple yes to something she hadn't dared dream of before, and now, she couldn't wait to begin.

Epilogue

Jess & Graham

It had taken her longer than she'd planned to get there with clinic meetings, hiring interviews, a surprise bout of spring flu cases, but she'd finally made it.

Just in time.

The winter snow had melted into spring puddles and February rains, but the twinkle lights on the gutters still blinked warm and slow, draped across the inn's eaves. Outside, the wind carried a chill, but inside the inn walls? It was everything she remembered: laughter tucked in corners, history stitched into every throw pillow, and the quiet shift of her pulse when she heard his voice drift from the kitchen.

Now, hours later, the girls were asleep, and the last guests were settled into their rooms with chocolate-covered strawberry trays and heart-shaped s'mores kits, while the parlor lights dimmed behind them.

Jess curled deeper into the Juniper Room quilt, one bare leg tangled with his, her hand tracing the curve of his shoulder where the softest flannel had been. Graham held her as if she'd never left—chest pressed to hers, palm resting low across her back.

"You beat the rain," he murmured in the hush between kisses. "Cupid's got good timing."

She laughed softly, her nose brushing his. "I don't know if it was Cupid. Felt more like divine intervention with a weather app."

"Let's not give Cupid the satisfaction," he said. "Guy gets around enough as it is."

Jess leaned in and kissed the corner of his mouth, slow and smiling. "Jealous of a cherub?"

"Definitely. He got to you first."

She pulled back just enough to look at him—hair mussed, temples damp, freckles mapped by firelight. "You had a bow and arrow all your own. Holiday playlists, heartfelt handmade ornaments, and pancakes perfectly sprinkled with chocolate chips."

"Don't forget the snowstorm," he said, brushing a thumb along her jaw. "Whole-house power outage's a pretty strong opener."

"Right," Jess said. "Start with survival. Then seduce."

"Classic strategy."

Her fingers slid across his ribs, then down—just enough to make his breath catch. "It worked."

His smile curved slowly. "I missed you."

"I missed you, too."

She moved closer to him then, brushing his legs as her body shifted across the mattress. Their skin touched in heat and silence; every touch infused with both freshness and something comfortably familiar. No hesitation, no rush, just the return of muscle memory and desire.

Graham's touch was gentle at first. His palms moved from her waist to her thighs, tracing the curve of her hips, then up again to where her breath caught beneath her ribs. She sighed into him, nails softly grazing down his back, her body arching as his kiss deepened.

"You're warm," he whispered into her neck.

"You're overheated," she said, tugging at the blanket to expose more of his chest.

He rolled them over smoothly, pinning her underneath him. Their eyes met, and he kissed her again—full, confident, and grateful.

They tumbled, tangled in laughter and love-drunk, with their limbs wrapping around and shifting, rediscovering the feel of home beneath their skin. Pillow-soft sighs filled the space between touch and breath, her name a hum against his jaw as she traced a path with her mouth to the hollow of his throat.

Somewhere between the second time and the laughter that followed, Jess leaned against his chest and finally caught her breath.

"You know," she whispered, legs still tangled with his, "for an inn with a Christmas legacy—"

He quirked a brow. "We throw one hell of a Valentine's Day?"

"Exactly."

He laughed, head falling back against the pillow. "We could rebrand it. 'Holly House—Now Serving Love Year-Round.'"

She buried her face in the crook of his arm. "As long as it still includes pancakes."

"Heart-shaped in February. Bunny-shaped in April. I'm ready."

She looked up, serious suddenly, one finger tracing the line of his jaw. "Thank you."

"For what?"

"For still being here."

"Thank you, for coming back."

He kissed her again.

And in the quiet of the old room, with the fire low and the wind softly brushing along the shutters, Jess curled into the crook of his arm. The quilt wrapped them like memory, and Holly House gently kept their secrets.

In another room, pink twinkle lights blinked over the hearth, leftover from Noelle's "Cupid Needs Glitter Hearts" decorating spree. Clara's careful schedule still hung beside the coffee bar, decorated with heart stickers.

Finally, Holly House hummed again with something sweeter than nostalgia.

It hummed with possibilities.

Love had arrived quietly, tucked inside snow flurries, sweet gingerbread, and child-like laughter beside a parlor fire.

And now, hand in hand, tangled beneath the same quilt that had once been stitched with someone else's dreams, Jess and Graham were writing the start of their own.

Through Cupid—or a weather app—they had found each other, and neither one was letting go.

Not this season.

Not the next one, either.

About Amber W. Lynne

An award-winning author from the misty, coffee-scented land-scapes of the Pacific Northwest, Amber blends slow-burn tension, heart-tugging emotion, and just the right amount of sweet and heat into every story she writes. The relationships are relatable and her heroines are fierce, independent, and (sometimes) a little stubborn, but they always find the right man to love them.

Fueled by caffeine and an unshakable belief in love, Amber has been crafting stories since childhood, drawn to the way romance can heal, challenge, and transform. When she's not writing, she's playing with her five kids (I KNOW!), helping fellow writers embrace their literary dreams, or spending time with her hubby making a love story of her own.

<u>Ways to stay in touch:</u>

- Subscribe to her Newsletter

- Via email: info@AmberWLynne.com

- Follow on Instagram - AmberLynne.Author

- Follow on Facebook - Amber W. Lynne, Author

Also by Amber W. Lynne

Working For Love

Lanyards & Lariats
Toolbelts & Ties
Spreadsheets & Sprinkles
Gowns & Gavels
Bourbons & Bling
Holly & Heartbeats

Leave a review at your favorite retailer, and sign-up for Amber's newsletter, to get more love stories, sneak peeks, a chance at Beta or ARC reads, and exclusive giveaways.

To find more books by Amber W. Lynne, visit:
https://amberlynneauthor.com

Lanyards & Lariats

Working for Love, Book 1

Visit https://AmberLynneAuthor.com and subscribe to our monthly newsletter to receive launch updates, sneak peeks, exclusive giveaways, and early access to beta and ARC reads!

Her father had won.

Bailey threw the morning paper down on the table, cussed, and then snatched it back up.

There she was—staring back from the front page. The photo was old: platinum-blonde curls framing her heart-shaped face, polished and pristine. It made her look way younger than her thirty-five years, but it also pissed her off. That girl wasn't her anymore.

Hugh "Rusty" Reynolds III, patriarch of the family, had decided that Sherry Ann Reynold's obituary would feature their perfect daughter. Did it even cross his mind to ask if she wanted her name—let alone her face—plastered across the front page?

Her mom had been planning for her death for over a year. From the orchids at the memorial to the canapes served at the wake, Sherry knew what she'd wanted. Although it wasn't cancer, she vowed to accept whatever came her way in life. Bailey had promised her mom a picture book perfect ending, but this felt like her father was violating her privacy. Hugh was more than aware that she didn't like the press.

Instead, the old coot let Sherry write whatever she wanted and then tied it up with a big fat bow for the papers. Rusty would do anything to make their family name look better. The obituary mentioned nothing about the funeral arrangements, but a brief note suggested that, instead of flowers, mourners could send gifts to a local homeless shelter.

Without information, she'd be calling Clinton, their family attorney. "No." She shook her head and threw the paper back down on the worn laminate table. Her truck keys lay in the basket at the table's center. Instead of reaching for the paper a third time, she grabbed them, took five steps to the door, and then fifteen to her truck.

It growled to life, and she was spitting gravel before she'd even pulled on her seatbelt. Music pumped from the radio. A heady mix of guitar and fiddle. The bass gave her a steady beat to focus on as she drove the old blue Ford F-150 down the dirt lane. The truck passed acre after acre of lush green farmland. All that grass and land was another part of her mother's legacy. One she'd been so glad to share with her daughter. A herd of cattle grazed on her left, and she honked at them. They didn't stop chewing to even notice her.

When the song stopped, replaced by an annoying announcer selling mattresses, she turned the radio off. Oppressive silence was worse than the radio commercial. Tires crunched and bit into the edge of the road. She turned the engine off. "You bastard!" she said, hitting the steering wheel. Over and over, she slammed her hand into the dash until her palm ached.

When she stopped, her hand was red, and her throat was raw. "Damn you." With a hand on each side, she dropped her forehead and gripped the steering wheel until her knuckles were white. The heat building up in the cab forced her to lift her head and turn the key. "Fine." She gritted her teeth, turned the truck back around, and drove home.

"Ms. Reynolds, I was hoping to speak with you sooner, but you never returned my calls."

"I stopped answering calls from lawyers after my ex tried to take me for everything I owned."

"And, as I remember it, you should be happily answering my calls and thanking me for what we pulled off."

"Whatever. A hack out of law school could have won that case. He cheated on me with half the women he met."

"Right, but he also had an ironclad prenuptial. Which, I'll remind you, I advised you not to sign."

"Thanks for the walk down memory lane, Clint, but that's not why I called."

He cleared his voice, and it rumbled across the line. "Clinton, or Mr. Conners, if you don't mind."

"Sure. You know why I called, Mr. Conners."

"It's truly unfortunate. You have my deepest sympathies." There were the muffled sounds of a woman's voice, and the rasping sound of paper shuffling. "Your mother has been...was...a client here for many years."

The kitchen wasn't large enough for her to pace. With a quick push, she shoved open the screen door and stepped onto the wrap-around porch. "Just lay it out."

"I have explicit instructions to wait."

"On what?" Her feet crunched in the rocky driveway and her voice startled the chickens nearby. Their squawks forced her around the backside of the house.

"You'll need to attend the memorial service and there will be a reading of your mother's Last Will and Testament on Friday."

The tire swing hanging off the tree in the old house's backyard rocked in the soft breeze. "This Friday? Like this week? But, I—"

"You knew this was coming, Ms. Reynolds. It would have helped if you'd answered my phone calls." He took a deep breath that whistled in her ear. "The memorial is Thursday afternoon, and the reading of the Will is the next morning."

"My contact info is the same. Send me the details and I'll be there." A rumbling in the distance caught her attention as she finished walking around the house. "I have to go."

He was sputtering on the line when she hung up, but she didn't have time to worry about being rude. As the large yellow bus rumbled up to the end of the driveway, she watched the doors open wide and her daughter bounced out. The afternoon light shimmered off the sun-kissed ponytail and sweet pink cheeks of the little girl that looked so much like her at that age.

"Hey Rosie, how was school?"

"The best!" she said, taking Bailey's outstretched hand.

She gripped her daughter's small hand and then took a deep breath. "Let's go get you a snack. We need to talk."

NOW AVAILABLE AT MAJOR BOOK RETAILERS

RECIPE: Holiday Morning Hash

Savory Stove-Top Casserole

Serves: 6–8
Prep Time: 15 min
Cook Time: 25–30 min

Born out of panic, perfected by hunger. This hearty, one-skillet breakfast is Jess's answer to no power, no oven, and a full house of hungry guests. It's warm, cheesy, and can be eaten with a fork or a mittened hand. Pair with strong coffee and general holiday chaos.

INGREDIENTS:

- 2 tablespoons butter or oil

- 1 small onion, diced

- 1 bell pepper, diced (optional, but festive)

- 1(1-pound) bag frozen shredded hash browns (thawed, if possible)

- 1 cup cooked sausage, bacon, or diced ham

- 6 large eggs

- 1/4 cup milk

- 1 1/2 cups shredded cheddar (or whatever cheese survived the fridge purge)

- Salt & pepper to taste

- Chopped scallions or parsley for garnish (optional)

INSTRUCTIONS:

1. In a large skillet or sauté pan, melt butter over medium heat. Sauté onion and bell pepper until soft, about 5 minutes.

2. Add hash browns and spread them evenly. Cook until lightly golden, flipping once or twice, about 10 minutes.

3. Stir in your cooked sausage, bacon, or ham.

4. In a bowl, whisk eggs with milk, salt, and pepper. Pour

over the hash brown mixture.

5. Reduce heat to low, cover, and cook gently until eggs
   are just set, 8–10 minutes.

6. Sprinkle with cheese, cover again, and let melt.

7. Garnish with herbs if you're feeling fancy!

**Serve warm, ideally with someone singing off-key carols
nearby.**

RECIPE: Jess's Christmas Eggnog

(This is the safe version!)

Serves: 6–8

Prep Time: 20 minutes + chilling

Let's just say Jess learned the hard way that not all holiday traditions age well! So, here's a safer, modern take—still creamy, cozy, and rich with nostalgia, minus the food poisoning risk. Cheers to second chances and properly pasteurized holiday cheer!

<u>INGREDIENTS:</u>

- 6 large egg yolks (pasteurized, if using raw)

- 3/4 cup granulated sugar

- 2 cups whole milk

- 1 cup heavy cream

- 1/2 teaspoon vanilla extract

- 1/2 teaspoon freshly grated nutmeg (plus more for serving)

- 1 cup bourbon, rum, or brandy (optional—but recommended for trauma recovery)

- Whipped cream or cinnamon sticks for garnish (if you're feeling fancy)

INSTRUCTIONS:

1. Whisk the yolks and sugar in a medium saucepan until thick and pale.

2. Add the milk and cream slowly, whisking constantly.

3. Heat gently over medium-low, stirring until the mixture reaches 160°F. (Use a candy thermometer if you've got one. If not, stop when it coats the back of a spoon.)

4. Remove from heat and stir in vanilla, nutmeg, and your spirit of choice.

5. Cool to room temp, then chill in the fridge for at least 4 hours (overnight is even better).

6. Serve cold, garnished with a dollop of whipped cream, a dusting of nutmeg, or a cinnamon stick for flair.

Also, tasty warm, but always best with family and friends!

www.ingramcontent.com/pod-product-compliance
Lightning Source LLC
Chambersburg PA
CBHW031527310726
48971CB00008B/2383